FUNNY STORIES FOR NINE YEAR OLDS

Helen Paiba is known as one of the most committed, knowledgeable and acclaimed children's booksellers in Britain. For more than twenty years she owned and ran the Children's Bookshop in Muswell Hill, London, which under her guidance gained a superb reputation for its range of children's books and for the advice available to its customers.

Helen was involved with the Booksellers Association for many years and served on both its Children's Bookselling Group and the Trade Practices Committee. In 1995 she was given honorary life membership of the Booksellers Association of Great Britain and Ireland in recognition of her outstanding services to the association and to the book trade. In the same year the Children's Book Circle (sponsored by Books for Children) honoured her with the Eleanor Farjeon Award, given for distinguished service to the world of children's books.

She retired in 1995 and now lives in London.

Titles available in this series

Funny Stories for Five Year Olds
Magical Stories for Five Year Olds
Animal Stories for Five Year Olds
Adventure Stories for Five Year Olds
Bedtime Stories for Five Year Olds

Funny Stories for Six Year Olds
Magical Stories for Six Year Olds
Animal Stories for Six Year Olds
Adventure Stories for Six Year Olds
Bedtime Stories for Six Year Olds

Funny Stories for Seven Year Olds
Scary Stories for Seven Year Olds
Animal Stories for Seven Year Olds
Adventure Stories for Seven Year Olds

Funny Stories for Eight Year Olds
Scary Stories for Eight Year Olds
Animal Stories for Eight Year Olds
Adventure Stories for Eight Year Olds

Funny Stories for Nine Year Olds
Scary Stories for Nine Year Olds
Animal Stories for Nine Year Olds
Adventure Stories for Nine Year Olds

Funny Stories for Ten Year Olds
Scary Stories for Ten Year Olds
Animal Stories for Ten Year Olds
Adventure Stories for Ten Year Olds

Coming Soon

Revolting Stories for Nine Year Olds
Revolting Stories for Ten Year Olds

Funny
STORIES
for Nine Year Olds

COMPILED BY HELEN PAIBA

ILLUSTRATED BY LYNNE CHAPMAN

MACMILLAN
CHILDREN'S BOOKS

First published 1999 by Macmillan Children's Books
a division of Macmillan Publishers Limited
25 Eccleston Place, London SW1W 9NF
Basingstoke and Oxford
www.macmillan.com

Associated companies throughout the world

ISBN 0 330 37491 5

This collection copyright © Helen Paiba 1999
Illustrations copyright © Lynne Chapman 1999

9 8

A CIP catalogue record for this book is available from
the British Library.

Typeset by SX Composing DTP, Rayleigh, Essex
Printed and bound in Great Britain by
Mackays of Chatham plc, Kent

Contents

The Balaclava Story

George Layton

Tony and Barry both had one. I reckon half the kids in our class had one. But I didn't. My mum wouldn't even listen to me.

"You're not having a balaclava! What do you want a balaclava for in the middle of summer?"

I must've told her about ten times why I wanted a balaclava.

"I want one so's I can join the Balaclava Boys . . ."

"Go and wash your hands for tea, and don't be so silly."

She turned away from me to lay the table, so I put the curse of the middle finger on her. This was pointing both your middle fingers at somebody when they weren't looking. Tony had started it when Miss Taylor gave him a hundred lines for flicking paper pellets at Jennifer Greenwood. He had to write out a hundred times: "I must not fire missiles because it is dangerous and liable to cause damage to someone's eye."

Tony tried to tell Miss Taylor that he hadn't fired a missile, he'd just flicked a paper pellet, but she threw a piece of chalk at him and told him to shut up.

"Don't just stand there – wash your hands."

"Eh?"

"Don't say 'eh', say 'pardon'."

"What?"

"Just hurry up, and make sure the dirt comes off in the water, and not on the towel, do you hear?"

Ooh, my mum. She didn't half go on sometimes.

"I don't know what you get up to at school. How do you get so dirty?"

I knew exactly the kind of balaclava I wanted. One just like Tony's, a sort of yellowy-brown. His dad had given it to him because of his earache. Mind you, he didn't like wearing it at first. At school he'd given it to Barry to wear and got it back before home-time. But all the other lads started asking if they could have a wear of it, so Tony took it back and said from then on nobody but him could wear it, not even Barry. Barry told him he wasn't bothered because he was going to get a balaclava of his own, and so did some of the other lads. And that's how it started – the Balaclava Boys.

It wasn't a gang really. I mean they didn't have meetings or anything like that. They just went round together wearing their balaclavas, and if you didn't have one you couldn't go around with them. Tony and Barry were my best friends, but because I didn't have a balaclava, they wouldn't let me go round with them. I tried.

"Aw, go on, Barry, let us walk round with you."

"No, you can't. You're not a Balaclava Boy."

"Aw, go on."

"No."

"Please."

I don't know why I wanted to walk round with them anyway. All they did was wander up and down the playground dressed in their rotten balaclavas. It was daft.

"Go on, Barry, be a sport."

"I've told you. You're not a Balaclava Boy. You've got to have a balaclava. If you get one, you can join."

"But I can't, Barry. My mum won't let me have one."

"Hard luck."

"You're rotten."

Then he went off with the others. I wasn't half fed up. All my friends were in the Balaclava Boys. All the lads in my class except me. Wasn't fair. The bell went for the next lesson – ooh heck, handicraft with Miseryguts Garnett – then it was home-time. All the Balaclava Boys were going in and I followed them.

"Hey Tony, do you want to go down the woods after school?"

"No, I'm going round with the Balaclava Boys."

"Oh."

Blooming Balaclava Boys. Why wouldn't *my mum buy me a balaclava*? Didn't she realize that I was losing all my friends, and just because she wouldn't buy me one?

"Eh, Tony, we can go goose-gogging – you know, by those great gooseberry bushes at the other end of the woods."

"I've told you, I can't."

"Yes, I know, but I thought you might want to go goose-gogging."

"Well, I would, but I can't."

I wondered if Barry would be going as well.

"Is Barry going round with the Balaclava Boys an' all?"

"Course he is."

"Oh."

Blooming balaclavas. I wish they'd never been invented.

"Why won't your mum get you one?"

"I don't know. She says it's daft wearing a balaclava in the middle of summer. She won't let me have one."

"I found mine at home up in our attic."

Tony unwrapped some chewing gum and asked me if I wanted a piece.

"No, thanks." I'd've only had to wrap it in my handkerchief once we got in the classroom. You couldn't get away with anything with Mr Garnett.

"Hey, maybe you could find one in your attic."

For a minute I wasn't sure what he was talking about.

"Find what?"

"A balaclava."

"No, we haven't even got an attic."

I didn't half find handicraft class boring. All that mucking about with compasses and rulers. Or else it was weaving, and you got all tangled up with balls of wool. I was no good at handicraft and Mr Garnett agreed with me. Today was worse than ever. We were painting pictures and we had to call it "My Favourite Story". Tony was painting *Noddy in Toyland*. I told him he'd get into trouble.

"Garnett'll do you."

"Why? It's my favourite story."

"Yes, but I don't think he'll believe you."

Tony looked ever so hurt.

"But honest. It's my favourite story. Anyway what are you doing?"

He leaned over to have a look at my favourite story.

"Have you read it, Tony?"

"I don't know. What is it?"

"It's *Robinson Crusoe*, what do you think it is?"

He just looked at my painting.

"Oh, I see it now. Oh yes, I get it now. I couldn't make it out for a minute. Oh yes, there's Man Friday behind him."

"Get your finger off, it's still wet. And that isn't Man Friday, it's a coconut tree. And you've smudged it."

We were using some stuff called poster paint, and I got covered in it. I was getting it everywhere, so I asked Mr Garnett if I could go for a wash. He gets annoyed when you ask to be excused, but he could see I'd got it all over my hands, so he said I could go, but told me to be quick.

7

The washbasins were in the boys' cloak-room just outside the main hall. I got most of the paint off and as I was drying my hands, that's when it happened. I don't know what came over me. As soon as I saw that balaclava lying there on the floor, I decided to pinch it. I couldn't help it. I just knew that this was my only chance. I've never pinched anything before – I don't think I have – but I didn't think of this as . . . well . . . I don't even like saying it, but . . . well, stealing. I just did it.

I picked it up, went to my coat, and put it in the pocket. At least I tried to put it in the pocket but it bulged out, so I pushed it down the inside of the sleeve. My head was throbbing, and even though I'd just dried my hands, they were all wet from sweating. If only I'd thought a bit first. But it all happened so quickly. I went back to the classroom, and as I was going in I began to realize what I'd done. I'd *stolen* a balaclava. I didn't even know whose it was, but as I stood in the doorway I couldn't believe I'd done it. If only I could go back. In fact I thought I would but then Mr Garnett told me to hurry up and sit down. As I was going back to my desk I felt as if all the lads knew what I'd done. How could they? Maybe somebody had seen me. No! Yes! How *could* they? They could. Of course they couldn't. No, course not. What if they did though? Oh heck.

I thought home-time would never come but when the bell did ring I got out as quick as I could. I was going to put the balaclava back before anybody noticed; but as I got to the cloakroom I heard Norbert Lightowler shout out that someone had pinched his balaclava. Nobody took much notice, thank goodness, and I heard Tony say to him that he'd most likely lost it. Norbert said he hadn't but he went off to make sure it wasn't in the classroom.

I tried to be casual and took my coat, but I didn't dare put it on in case the balaclava popped out of the sleeve. I said tarah to Tony.

"Tarah, Tony, see you tomorrow."

"Yeh, tarah."

Oh, it was good to get out in the open air. I couldn't wait to get home and get rid of that blooming balaclava. Why had I gone and done a stupid thing like that? Norbert Lightowler was sure to report it to the Headmaster, and there'd be an announcement about it at morning assembly and the culprit would be asked to own up. I was running home as fast as I could. I wanted to stop and take out the balaclava and chuck it away, but I didn't dare. The faster I ran, the faster my head was filled with thoughts. I could give it back to Norbert.

You know, say I'd taken it by mistake. No, he'd never believe me. None of the lads would believe me. Everybody knew how much I wanted to be a Balaclava Boy. I'd have to get rid of the blooming thing as fast as I could.

My mum wasn't back from work when I got home, thank goodness, so as soon as I shut the front door, I put my hand down the sleeve of my coat for the balaclava. There was nothing there. That was funny, I was sure I'd put it down that sleeve. I tried down the other sleeve, and there was still nothing there. Maybe I'd got the wrong coat. No, it was my coat all right. Oh, blimey, I must've lost it while I was running home. I was glad in a way. I was going to have to get rid of it, now it was gone. I only hoped nobody had seen it drop out, but, oh, I was glad to be rid of it. Mind you, I was dreading going to school next morning. Norbert'll probably have reported it by now. Well, I wasn't going to own up. I didn't mind the cane, it wasn't that, but if you owned up, you had to go up on the stage in front of the whole school. Well, I was going to

11

forget about it now and nobody would ever know that I'd pinched that blooming lousy balaclava.

I started to do my homework, but I couldn't concentrate. I kept thinking about assembly next morning. What if I went all red and everybody else noticed? They'd know I'd pinched it then. I tried to think about other things, nice things. I thought about bed. I just wanted to go to sleep. To go to bed and sleep. Then I thought about my mum; what she'd say if she knew I'd been stealing. But I still couldn't forget about assembly next day. I went into the kitchen and peeled some potatoes for my mum. She was ever so pleased when she came in from work and said I must've known she'd brought me a present.

"Oh, thanks. What've you got me?"

She gave me a paper bag and when I opened it I couldn't believe my eyes – a blooming balaclava.

"There you are, now you won't be left out and you can stop making my life a misery."

"Thanks, Mum."

If only my mum knew she was making *my* life a misery. The balaclava she'd bought me was just like the one I'd pinched. I felt sick. I didn't want it. I couldn't wear it now. If I did, everybody would say it was Norbert Lightowler's. Even if they didn't, I just couldn't wear it. I wouldn't feel it was mine. I had to get rid of it. I went outside and put it down the lavatory. I had to pull the chain three times before it went away. It's a good job we've got an outside lavatory or else my mum would have wondered what was wrong with me.

I could hardly eat my tea.

"What's wrong with you? Aren't you hungry?"

"No, not much."

"What've you been eating? You've been eating sweets, haven't you?"

"No, I don't feel hungry."

"Don't you feel well?"

"I'm all right."

I wasn't, I felt terrible. I told my mum I was going upstairs to work on my model aeroplane.

"Well, it's my bingo night, so make yourself some cocoa before you go to bed."

I went upstairs to bed, and after a while I fell asleep. The last thing I remember was a big balaclava, with a smiling face, and it was the Headmaster's face.

I was scared stiff when I went to school next morning. In assembly it seemed different. All the boys were looking at me. Norbert Lightowler pushed past and didn't say anything. When prayers were finished I just stood there waiting for the Headmaster to ask for the culprit to own up, but he was talking about the school fête. And then he said he had something very important to announce and I could feel myself going red. My ears were burning like anything and I was going hot and cold both at the same time.

"I'm very pleased to announce that the school football team has won the inter-league cup . . ."

And that was the end of assembly, except that we were told to go and play in the schoolyard until we were called in, because

there was a teachers' meeting. I couldn't
understand why I hadn't been found out yet,
but I still didn't feel any better, I'd probably be
called to the Headmaster's room later on.

I went out into the yard. Everybody was
happy because we were having extra play-
time. I could see all the Balaclava Boys going
round together. Then I saw Norbert
Lightowler was one of them. I couldn't be
sure it was Norbert Lightowler because he
had a balaclava on, so I had to go up close to
him. Yes, it was Norbert. He must have
bought a new balaclava that morning.

"Have you bought a new one then,
Norbert?"

"Y'what?"

"You've bought a new balaclava, have
you?"

"What are you talking about?"

"Your balaclava. You've got a new
balaclava, haven't you?"

"No, I never lost it at all. Some fool had
shoved it down the sleeve of my raincoat."

Nat and the Great Bath Climb

Penelope Lively

The life of a young woodlouse is a very different matter to that of a young mouse. Mice are free and easy creatures compared to woodlice. Young mice are warned and scolded, but they also get away with a good deal, since their parents are skittish creatures themselves who enjoy a bit of fun and like to get the best out of life. Woodlice are another matter; their way of life is as stiff and awkward as their appearance. They have an outlook on life which is all their own – as indeed do most of us, but people tend to ignore that in the case of something with a top view like a very small armadillo and fourteen legs, which is why Mrs Dixon was so silly as to scream whenever she saw one. The woodlice had to put up with a great deal more from Mrs Dixon – and the rest of the Dixons – than she did from them.

The woodlice at fifty-four Pavilion Road lived in several large colonies. They preferred damp and murky places – the corner behind the sink where a dripping tap had made an area of moist and flaking plaster, the cupboard in the cloakroom where mildew grew on the Dixons' winter boots, the waste pipe of the bath.

The waste pipe was considered a particularly attractive habitat. Admittedly two or three times each day a Niagara Falls of soapy water came hurtling down and many a woodlouse had hurtled down with it and had to climb up again some fifteen feet from the drain outside. But woodlice are sturdy, uncomplaining creatures and they took this as part of the price one had to pay for a home that was forever dark, forever damp and forever undisturbed by mops and vacuum cleaners. The waste pipe had in fact several cracks and faulty joins through which they could climb out into the wall when threatened by bathwater. More than that, it gave them a magnificent opportunity to do what woodlice do.

Woodlice colonies are governed by Chief Woodlice, who are stern and ancient creatures with whiskers of immense length. Young woodlice are kept under the most strict control by their elders; indeed they are quite literally trampled on until large enough to hold their own. Woodlice are not creatures who go in much for expressing themselves or being original or striking out; one woodlouse acts and thinks much like another and this is the way the old woodlice want to keep it.

From time to time the Chief Woodlouse would call the whole colony together for a meeting. The object of this meeting was for the Chief Woodlouse to lecture the newest generation of young woodlice, who were allowed to attend as soon as their whiskers were three millimetres long, which meant they were grown-up.

The hero of this story, who was called Nat, came to his first such meeting when he was three weeks old – which in human terms is about eighteen years. The young woodlice sat in a row in the front, feeling important but nervous, while their parents and aunts and uncles crowded behind them and the Chief Woodlouse took up a position in front.

The Chief Woodlouse looked sternly down at the assembled crowd and began to speak. "We are gathered together today," he said, "to remind ourselves of the purpose of life." He glared at the young woodlice. "And what is the purpose of life?" The young woodlice, who knew they were not supposed to answer, gazed at him respectfully.

"The purpose of life is to climb up the side of the bath. That is what we are here for. That is why we were born. No one has ever succeeded. But the purpose of life is to try. Each and every one of us. Your turn has now come. Your mothers and fathers have tried before you. Some brave spirits have tried several times. All have failed."

There was a silence. The young woodlice gazed at the Chief Woodlouse and felt even more nervous and important. All except Nat, who was the youngest and smallest and had been in trouble most of his life for asking too many questions. Nat was thinking.

"You will make your attempts turn and turn about, starting with the eldest. Each of you will fail, but will have made a glorious attempt. You will then have your names inscribed on the Roll of Honour."

The young woodlice went quite pink with pride and excitement, all except Nat, who raised one of his fourteen legs. "Please, sir," he said, "why do we have to climb up the side of the bath?"

There was a gasp of horror from the crowd of woodlice. Nat's mother fainted clean away; his father bent his head in shame.

The Chief Woodlouse stared at Nat. His whiskers twitched in fury. "WHAT DID YOU SAY?"

Nat cleared his throat and repeated, politely and clearly, "Why do we have to climb up the side of the bath?"

The Chief Woodlouse huffed and puffed; his little black eyes bulged; he creaked with indignation. "BECAUSE IT'S THERE!" he roared and there was a rustle of agreement from the crowd of woodlice. Some of the youngsters turned to look reprovingly at Nat. His mother recovered from her faint and moaned that she would never get over the disgrace, never.

Nat sat tight. He said nothing more. He kept his thoughts to himself.

The young woodlice made their assaults upon the side of the bath alone. Each in turn would struggle up through the plughole and vanish from sight. Some while later – much later, sometimes – they would crawl back down again in a state of exhaustion. One or two said with shy pride that they had got six inches before they fell back. The unluckiest of all did not crawl back into the plughole but tumbled back in a torrent of water, having been spotted by Mrs Dixon. One after another they tried, and one after another they returned, beaten but content. When it came to Nat's turn his parents and relatives gathered round him and told him severely that this was his chance to make a man of himself and become exactly like everyone else. "Try hard," they told him, "and fail magnificently, and we shall be proud of you."

Nat looked upwards. Bright light, which

hurt his eyes, came through the plughole. He hauled himself up and out. It was dazzlingly bright out there and, for a few moments, he could see nothing but the glitter of the chrome circle on which he was standing. He felt terrifyingly exposed. Then he looked round and saw the whole immense smooth white length of the bath reaching away before him. It was even more enormous than people had said – it seemed to go on for ever, and if he looked to right or to left its sides towered upwards, first sloping and then absolutely sheer, up and up as far as you could see.

Nat walked out a few steps. It was very slippery. Even on the flat his legs slithered about. He toiled across to one side and gradually the smooth hard surface began to slope. He slithered even more. He slithered back to where he had started.

He looked at those white cliffs. Of course you couldn't climb them. That was the whole point.

He struggled a little way up the slope again.

Then he lost his grip and rolled down to the bottom.

Stuff this, thought Nat. *I'm not carrying on with this lark.* He sat down where he was and looked around him. The bath was a very boring place, he decided – either flat white or steep white and with nothing to look at. There was one of Mr Dixon's hairs, which to Nat was like a length of rope but not very interesting. There was also a grain of Mrs Dixon's bath salts which he tried to eat; it tasted nasty so he spat it out. He thought about going back down the plug hole; he could say – truthfully enough – that he had tried to climb up the side of the bath, and failed. He could have his name inscribed on the Roll of Honour, like everyone else. The idea of that was as boring as the scenery of the bath.

"Well!" said a voice. "Get on with it, then! Strive and struggle! Press on! Wear yourself out! That's what you're here for, isn't it?"

Nat looked all round. He could see no one.

"What's the matter?" continued the voice.

"Where's your grit and determination?"

Nat looked up. Far above him, on the distant heights of the right-hand side of the bath, he saw some legs. The legs twitched, took a few neat steps downwards, and a large spider came into view.

"Go on," said the spider, "climb. Give me something to laugh at."

"I'm not going to," said Nat. "There's no point. We can't."

The spider let out a length of thread and swung itself down until it was hanging halfway down the side of the bath. "Good grief! The first one of you with his head screwed on right. Too right you can't. I, on the other hand . . ." It gripped the side of the bath for a moment, and then swarmed up its thread and reappeared at the top. "Neat, eh?"

"Terrific," said Nat. "What is it like up there?"

"Truth to tell," said the spider, "there's not all that much to it. Quite a nice view. Come and see."

Nat stared. "But . . ." he began.

"Wait," ordered the spider. It raised its two rear legs and began to spin a great length of thread, which streamed out and came floating down until the end of it reached Nat in the bottom of the bath. "Take hold," instructed the spider. "Hang on tight."

Nat gripped the thread, which was sticky and felt slightly elastic but strong. The spider became very busy with its eight legs and Nat felt himself being slowly towed up the slope of the bath. He clung on for dear life. The spider continued to reel in the thread and Nat found himself rising up the sheer white wall. He swung around alarmingly and once or twice was bumped against the side. "Fend off," advised the spider. "Use your feet. Not much further."

Up went Nat. He did not dare look down. Once, he thought, *I am doing what no other woodlouse has ever done.*

"There!" said the spider. "Piece of cake, isn't it?"

Nat found himself standing on a white cliff-top. He walked to the far edge and looked out

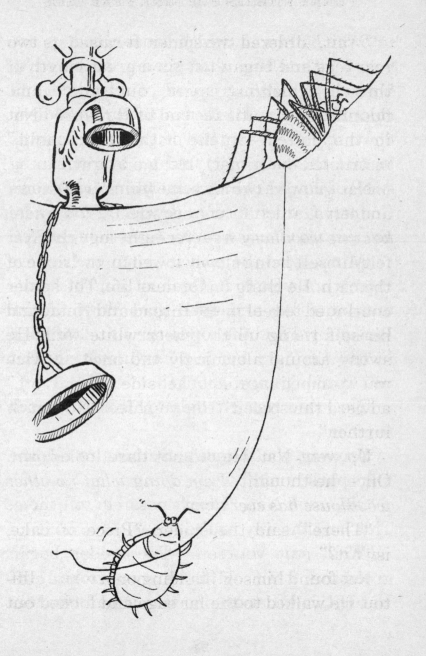

into the bathroom, which, since woodlice are better at smelling than seeing, appeared to him as a dizzying scene of distance and colourful blurs. There was a terrifying drop down to a great expanse of green (which was in fact the bath mat) and an overwhelming smell of flowers (which came from Mrs Dixon's Country Garden talcum powder). *I am where no other woodlouse has ever been*, thought Nat.

"Mind," said the spider, "once you're here there's not a lot to it. One just kind of hangs out for a bit and then goes down again. Personally I find the top of the standard lamp in the sitting room more exhilarating. But you wouldn't know about that."

"No," said Nat. He didn't think he wanted to either.

"Anyway, you'll have something to tell the folks back home."

"No," said Nat. "I can't possibly tell them. This isn't the way you're supposed to do it."

"Well, suit yourself." The spider began grooming itself with its two front legs. Nat noticed that on one side it had two legs that were very much shorter than the others.

"What happened to your legs?" he asked. He had often seen spiders before but he had never been on such close terms with one and, as we know, he was fond of asking questions.

"Nosy fellow, aren't you?" said the spider. "I had a slight difference of opinion with a friend, as it happens. Quite good fun at the time."

It was a ferocious-looking creature. You'd do well to stay on the right side of it, Nat thought.

"How about a quick spin down to the bath mat and up to the laundry basket?" continued the spider.

Nat thanked it but said he thought he ought to be getting back now. The spider spun a short length of thread, Nat took hold of it, and the spider lowered him slowly over the side and down into the bath again. When he got to the bottom Nat gave the thread a tug, as he had been instructed, let go of it, and the spider reeled it back in again. Then it peered down over the edge and called, "Well, cheerio then. See you around, I dare say."

"Cheerio," called Nat, "and thanks very much. I enjoyed it."

"Don't mention it," said the spider. "Take care. Don't do anything I wouldn't do."

Nat trudged back down the length of the bath. He slithered across the chrome of the plug hole and down into the dark, homely hole. He crawled down the damp, familiar pipe and when he got to the first bend there was a reception committee of woodlice waiting for him, headed by the Chief Woodlouse.

"You have tried to climb up the side of the bath?" said the Chief Woodlouse, in his most stern and dreadful tones.

"Yes, sir," said Nat.

"And you have failed?"

"Yes, sir," said Nat.

"Then," said the Chief Woodlouse, "I shall inscribe your name on the Roll of Honour. From now on you are exactly the same as every other woodlouse. Be proud of it."

"Yes, sir," said Nat.

And being a sensible fellow, he kept to himself for ever after the fact that he had been where no woodlouse had ever been before.

Ivan's Shadow

A Story from Russia

Marcus Crouch

The old folk had three sons to care for them. Two were good lads, always busy watching their sheep in the fields. The third son – well, he was called Ivanushko and he was as useless as his brothers were useful. He spent most of his days lying on the stove, whistling and catching flies.

One day Mother made dumplings and told Ivanushko to take them to his brothers for dinner. She packed them neatly in a pot, and he picked it up and ambled off, not hurrying too much for it was still early and he needed to save his strength for the rest of the day.

It was a lovely day. The sun shone brightly,

and Ivan's shadow moved along at his side. After a while he noticed this, and he thought to himself in his dim way: *Who is this fellow? I don't know him. I wonder why he sticks so close. Perhaps the poor lad is hungry. Here, have a dumpling.* He tossed one at the shadow, but it kept going beside him. He threw it more dumplings. Still it didn't go away. *What a pig!* Thought Ivan, and gave it the rest of his load. Still it followed him, and in disgust Ivan threw the pot at it and this smashed to pieces.

When he got to his brothers they said: "Where's our dinner?"

"Well, brothers, I was bringing it, but some stranger followed me and kept asking for food, so in the end he had the lot."

"What stranger?"

"Why, this black fellow. See, he's still by my side."

The brothers fell into a rage and gave Ivanushko a fearful beating. He went home as puzzled as he was hurt. Whoever could that black man be?

Another time, when it was coming up to Christmas, Ivan's parents sent him to town in a cart to buy what was needed for the feast. Ivan set off, cracking his whip proudly and singing a cheerful song. He had a fine time in the market, buying all sorts of things: different kinds of food, cups and plates and knives, and a big table.

It made a heavy load. On the way home the old horse began to labour under the weight and wheezed and panted. *Poor Dobbin!* Thought Ivan. *How can I help him? I know; that table has as many legs as the horse. It can surely make its own way home.* So he threw the table out into the road and drove on.

There were many birds, flying low over the cart and calling in their high voices. "Poor things," said Ivan to himself. "They must be starving." He stopped the cart, got down and laid out plates in the road. He piled these high with food, and shouted: "Eat up, little ones; you deserve Christmas just as much as us." And he cracked his whip and set the horse going again.

The road ran through a plantation of young trees. There had been a fire and many of the trees were burnt down to stumps. *Oh dear!* thought Ivan. *Those little fellows have no hats. They will catch cold, as sure as my name's whatever it is.* Again he stopped, and covered as many stumps as he could with cups and pots.

Ivan was feeling very happy. He had done many good deeds already that day and he longed to do more. When he came to a stream he thought he would give the old horse a treat, so he took the beast out of the shafts and led him to the water for a drink. The horse was not thirsty and took no notice. "What's the matter? Don't you like the taste?" said Ivan. "Perhaps you would rather have salt in it." He took out the big bag he had bought and poured the lot into the stream. Still the horse would not drink. "Drink, you selfish old bag-of-bones!" shouted Ivan angrily, and he picked up the branch of a tree and hit the horse on the head with it. The old horse just dropped dead.

Ivan looked in the cart. Of all the goods he had bought in the town only a bag of spoons was left. He picked up the bag and slung it over his shoulder, and began to walk the rest of the way home. As he lumbered on his way the spoons rattled against one another, making a chattering noise. To Ivanushko it sounded as if the spoons were saying "Silly Ivan! Silly Ivan!"

"So that's what you think," he shouted in a temper. He flung the bag on the ground and jumped on it, screaming: "That will teach you to be rude."

The family were waiting for him when he got home. "Where's everything?" they said.

"Hasn't the table got here yet?" asked Ivan. "I left it on the road and was sure it would get home first. The birds are using the plates. I left the cups and pots for those poor hatless trees. The old horse wanted the salt to flavour the water, and as for the spoons, they didn't deserve to be carried so I left them to take care of themselves."

"Where is the horse?"

"He had a headache, so I had to leave him behind with the cart."

The brothers could put up with their little brother no longer. They talked about what they should do with Ivan, and decided that they must get rid of him once and for all. One day when he was dozing by the stove they grabbed hold of him and stuffed him into a sack. They carried him to the river. It was frozen hard, so they left him on the bank while they went to look for a hole in the ice.

After a while Ivan heard the jingling of harness, and a rich man came by in his fine horse-sleigh. Ivan began to struggle in his sack, shouting: "I won't do it! I won't do it!"

"What won't you do?" asked the rich man.

"They are going to make me governor of a province, and I don't want it. What do I know about ruling and handing out justice?"

"I know all about that," said the rich man. "I wouldn't mind being a governor. We had better change places."

He let Ivanushko out of the sack and crawled in himself. Ivan tied it tightly. Then he took the sleigh and cracked his whip, and away went the three big horses. Soon the brothers came back and picked up the sack. They carried it, puffing and panting, until they came to a hole. They dropped their burden through the ice, and it went: *Bubble! Bubble!* out of sight.

The brothers started homeward, half glad to be rid of their tiresome brother, half ashamed of what they had done. There was a jingling sound, and along came Ivanushko,

cracking his whip and singing at the top of his voice. "What do you think of my river horses?" he shouted. "They are the pick of the underwater stable. Gee up, my beauties!" And they watched him out of sight.

Anyone for a Banana?

John Agard

One of those grey, wet London days, when you could disappear into your coat or anorak, a girl named Shona was travelling with her dad on the Underground.

Nobody seemed to be in a talking or smiling mood, so Shona whispered to her dad, "Why is everybody so serious?"

She didn't know what it was to whisper easy. She whispered loud enough to make one man in a bowler hat look up from his newspaper.

"Must be all the tension and the cold," her dad said.

"What's tension?" Shona asked.

"Pressure," her dad said. "Big city pressure."

She saw her dad smile as he said "big city pressure", and she could tell from the look behind his silver-framed specs that he must be making up some story in his head.

Shona's dad was from the island of St Kitts in the Caribbean and he was always telling her stories. Once, when she couldn't get to sleep, he got her to count the beads in her hair. Beads like smiling seeds all over her plaited hair. "Better than counting sheep," he told her.

But right now, Shona was counting how many more stops they had left. Shona's school was near Wood Green, which was a long way on the Piccadilly Line. Her dad was taking her to school after a visit to the dentist. There were at least another nine stops to go, and Shona wished that something interesting would brighten up the long journey.

A punk got on. At least, he looked like a

punk to Shona because he had pink spiky hair and a denim jacket that said DRACULA RULES OK on it.

He sat down next to the Bowler-Hat-Man, who was still reading his newspaper.

Punk-Boy lit a cigarette, and started smoking.

Bowler-Hat-Man turned to him and said, "No smoking on the Underground, if you don't mind."

"Me mouth mightn't be allowed to smoke, but who says me ear can't?"

With that, Punk-Boy put the cigarette into his ear like a circus act, and a stream of smoke wriggled up past his spiky hair.

Shona thought he looked really funny with his fowlcock hairstyle and the smoke coming out of his ear. But nobody laughed, and Bowler-Hat-Man said again to Punk-Boy: "Some of us care about our lungs, you know. If you must pollute the air, would you kindly go elsewhere?"

"Sorry, mate," Punk-Boy said. "Disgusting habit, I agree." He stubbed out the cigarette on the tip of his boot and put it back in his jacket pocket.

The train came to a stop. Doors as usual sliding open. Doors as usual sliding shut. People as usual getting off. People as usual getting on.

It wasn't busy like it was in the rush hour, so at least the train wasn't packed. Shona hated it when everybody was squashed together. Maybe that's why they called it the Tube, she thought. Like a squashy tube of toothpaste.

At the next stop, Green Park, two teenage boys got on. One was white, and he was holding a big stereo with loud music coming through.

The other was black, and he was holding a skateboard under one arm.

Stereo-Boy began to turn up the volume of his tape recorder, while his friend, Skateboard-Boy, said, "Yeah, pump up the volume, pump up the volume."

Shona had heard this song on Top of the Pops. It had a good beat.

Punk-Boy started shaking his head to the music, his spiky hair bobbing from side to side.

"Pump up the volume. Nice it up. Wicked," Skateboard-Boy said, trying to balance on his skateboard at the same time as the train was moving.

A woman looked up from her magazine and raised her eyebrows.

Bowler-Hat-Man raised his eyebrows too, then he coughed and went on reading his newspaper.

Maybe that's what music does to some grown-ups, Shona thought. *Some tap their feet. Some nod their chins. Some close their eyes. Some just raise their eyebrows or cough*.

And that's exactly what Bowler-Hat-Man did. He coughed again and raised his eyebrows.

An old lady, sitting next to Shona's dad, kept stroking the ear of the small mousy-faced dog whimpering on her lap. "Never mind, Bessie," the old lady was saying to comfort the dog, "Never mind. It's only music. It won't hurt yah."

"Call that music?" Bowler-Hat-Man said. "Sounds more like a noise-box to me. It's upset even the blooming dog."

"This ain't no noise-box." Stereo-Boy turned to Bowler-Hat-Man. "This, for your information, mate, is a Brixton Briefcase."

Skateboard-Boy burst out laughing, and Bowler-Hat-Man frowned.

"Whatever you call it, dearie," the old lady said with a thin-lip smile, "please, not so loud. Bessie appreciates her music soft."

Stereo-Boy turned down the music very very low, more out of consideration for the old lady and her dog than for anything Bowler-Hat-Man had said.

It was then they all realized that for some reason or other the train had stalled up.

The train just wasn't moving. They were neither going forward nor backward. They were stuck, yes, stuck in the Underground tunnel, and nobody could say how long they'd be like that.

Bowler-Hat-Man kept looking at his watch.

One passenger got up and walked through

the connecting door into another carriage.

Shona had travelled before on trains that stopped in the middle of an Underground tunnel, but never for such a long time.

After ten minutes or so, the train was still stuck. There wasn't anything the passengers could do but wait.

"Hope it ain't some accident causing the delay," her dad said. "You're missing enough school as it is. All we can do is wait."

But it was boring just sitting there in the stuffy-up Underground.

If Bowler-Hat-Man hadn't been such a spoilsport, Shona thought, she could have asked Stereo-Boy to put the music back on. She was sure the old lady wouldn't have minded.

Right now, Stereo-Boy was arguing with his friend Skateboard-Boy about which brand of trainers was the best. They didn't seem too bothered by the train being stalled up, though Skateboard-Boy sucked his teeth once or twice.

Shona took out a packet of bubblegum

from her anorak pocket and began chewing away.

Punk-Boy put on a silly posh voice like one of those actors doing a comic impression on telly. "I say, this is a no-bubblegum-chewing carriage, I'm afraid. Kindly go elsewhere if you must pollute the air with your bubbles." He said it just the way Bowler-Hat-Man had said, "No smoking on the Underground, if you don't mind."

Bowler-Hat-Man shifted in his seat but Shona knew Punk-Boy was only joking.

The old lady stroked the ear of her small dog. "Won't be long, Bessie, won't be long," she kept telling her.

Just then, the connecting door separating their carriage from the next one was opened, and in walked a very short old man with a yellow umbrella. Yellow socks were peeping out from under his grey trousers, and a yellow handkerchief was tucking out from his grey coat pocket.

The old man sat down without a word, hands propped on the handle of the yellow umbrella, and began whistling softly to himself.

Shona thought he looked a bit spooky, in a friendly sort of way. But maybe he was just an ordinary old man who saw so much grey around him – grey clouds, grey buildings, grey coats – that he decided to bring touches of yellow into his life. He even had a yellow scarf round his neck. Next to his grey coat it took on a special sunflower brightness.

All the while he sat there, the old man kept up his soft whistling. Nobody made any comment, not even Bowler-Hat-Man.

The people round him were trying their best not to make contact with his eyes because they didn't know what the old man might get up to.

Apart from the old man's whistling, nothing was happening. It was like waiting to see the dentist.

Then Punk-Boy pointed to the bright yellow scarf, and just for fun he asked the old man which football team he supported.

"I support the joy of life, my young friend,

but I don't suppose you've heard of that team." The old man spoke in a highish sing-song sort of voice. "My name is Doctor Bananas, and I never travel in a no-laughing carriage. I whistle to myself. Don't need a ticket to whistle to yourself, do you?"

Nobody said anything.

"Heard of the monkey who went bananas in space?" the old man asked, all of a sudden. "Serves them right for putting a monkey in a spaceship. Should have asked the monkey's permission. Should have consulted old Doctor Bananas, shouldn't they? Had a go at the control panel and all, our monkey did. After all, that's what buttons are for. To be pushed. Are there any bananas on Mars, I ask you? Well, then, only God has the right to pick the bananas that grow in space. They're poisoning the fish, they're poisoning the seals, now they're after the bananas in space. Let them be. And like I always say, a banana a day keeps the doctor away . . ."

The old man spoke very quickly, as if he didn't need to pause for breath. Then he

49

pulled out his handkerchief and shook it in the air. Out of nowhere a banana appeared in his hand, and there, back in his coat pocket, was the yellow handkerchief. It was like a magic show, and Shona was certain that this Doctor Bananas must be some kind of magician.

He peeled the banana carefully, ate it, and put the skin into his coat pocket.

"I always take my litter home with me. Do you?" he asked, suddenly turning to Bowler-Hat-Man, who looked completely caught by surprise.

"I should jolly well say I do," was all Bowler-Hat-Man said.

"And I should jolly well hope so," Doctor Bananas said, pointing his umbrella towards Bowler-Hat-Man. The way he was pointing that yellow umbrella, you'd think it was some kind of magic wand or that he was about to conduct some kind of orchestra with it.

"Well, must be on my way to visit some of the other folks stuck on a train in the middle of a tunnel, neither going forward nor backward. Neither going up nor down. Nothing to do but wait. Nothing to do but face each other. Good bananas to you, my friends. Good bananas till we meet again."

And just so, Doctor Bananas disappeared into the next carriage.

"Well, it takes all sorts to make a world," said the old lady with the dog.

"He sounded bananas to me," said Punk-

Boy. "Only wish the geezer could have done some magic to get the train moving."

But Shona had her eyes on Bowler-Hat-Man, for all of a sudden he wasn't looking very well. He put one hand to his forehead as if he could feel a headache coming on. Maybe the Underground was becoming too stuffy for him, or he was tired of waiting for the train to start.

"I'm beginning to feel a bit claustrophobic," said Bowler-Hat-Man, taking out a yellow handkerchief from his coat pocket and fanning away. "I must say, the lack of air is driving me absolutely bananas."

Shona offered him some bubblegum, but Bowler-Hat-Man said a polite, "No thank you."

"Then would you like my dad to tell you a story?" Shona suggested. "He's good at telling scary jumbie stories."

"No thank you," Bowler-Hat-Man said again, this time with a slight suggestion of a smile. But before you could say crick-crack, Shona's dad had begun a West Indian jumbie story about a certain Jack-a-Lantern, who at nights would make people lose their way with a mysterious yellow light.

"That's awfully nice of you to tell me a story," said Bowler-Hat-Man, "but a ghost story isn't exactly what I need just now, thank you."

"Well, how about a little music?" suggested Skateboard-Boy. "Pump up the volume!"

Stereo-Boy didn't need any more prompting from Skateboard-Boy to start the music going again, and this time Bowler-Hat-Man didn't object. In fact, he turned to the old lady with the dog and said, "I see your Bessie isn't too bothered by the music now. She's even wagging her tail."

"Takes time," replied the old lady. "But I always knew my Bessie had an ear for music. You do, don't you, Bessie?"

Then Bowler-Hat-Man actually reached across and tickled Bessie behind the ears. "I don't know what's come over me," he said. "But then I never did like being enclosed. I do hope the train gets going. Besides, I'm beginning to feel a bit hungry. Haven't eaten since lunch. That reminds me, a banana a day keeps the doctor away." With that, Bowler-Hat-Man opened the briefcase on his knees. The last thing anybody expected him to produce was a huge yellow banana, but that's exactly what happened. Bowler-Hat-Man took out a big banana and started eating it as carefully as he had folded his newspaper.

"I never leave my litter lying around," he said, putting the skin back inside his briefcase.

"Anyone for a banana?" he asked, looking round the carriage, and producing yet another banana from his briefcase.

"How many bananas you got in there, mate?" asked Punk-Boy.

"You never know, my young friend, you never know. Life is full of surprises. There may even be bananas on Mars, for all we know. Don't suppose any of you would care to join me, as the monkey said when he went bananas in outer space?"

Suddenly Shona began giggling, because

Bowler-Hat-Man looked so funny sitting there in his pinstriped suit, carefully munching a banana, and just as carefully putting the skin back inside his briefcase.

Nobody seemed to mind any more that the train had been stuck in the tunnel for fifteen minutes, for situations like these seem to get people talking to each other.

Soon the sound of laughter flooded the train and echoed down the tunnel.

When at last the train was on the move again, Bowler-Hat-Man was ready to get off at the next stop, King's Cross.

"Good Lord," he said suddenly. "That old man must have forgotten his umbrella." And he gave Shona a funny look, as if they were sharing a secret.

Then, with a very dignified "Good bananas to you, everybody", Bowler-Hat-Man went off into the crowd, holding in one hand his leather briefcase, and in the other a bright yellow umbrella.

The Reluctant Dragon and the Wilful Princess

William Raeper

Reginald lolled back and puffed out his scaly chest. "Oh – oh – umm!" he yawned, licking his hard, shiny lips. "Such a delicious day."

The daisies were drowsy in the heat, their faces pointed sleepily towards the sun, and nearby a careless brook tinkled over a myriad of coloured pebbles. Reginald pared a solitary claw and rolled his large, bulging eyes round in his head. Sleep had refreshed his limbs and the scents of summer filled his smoky nostrils.

"This is the life!" he hummed to himself. "This is the Life!" and a little shower of sparks tumbled from his mouth on to the grass.

Reginald was, you see, a dragon. Not a dragon of the old school who burned up villages and terrorized young maidens, but a dragon of the new school who did nothing at all. He practised a little flying before dinner perhaps, or roasted the occasional animal, but he attempted nothing too strenuous – or barbaric. He lived in the well of a pleasant valley that was pleasantly warm in summer and pleasantly cool in winter. He had a cave to snuggle in and a hoard of treasure to guard. He was completely and peacefully content, if pricked at times by an uncomfortable feeling of boredom. Reginald had lived in the valley longer than even he could remember, and although there had been a time when he had been fierce – gushing fire all over helpless men and innocent forests – he had not done anything of that kind for hundreds of years.

I could lie here for ever, thought Reginald dreamily to himself. *The sunlight is like very nectar*. And plucking a daisy (which had been minding its own business) in one shiny claw, Reginald set himself to contemplate the beauties of nature for a while.

He had just wrinkled his eyes shut, and a thin column of smoke was rising from his nose in a doze, when he awoke with a start to find himself covered in a huge black shadow. Reginald shivered. Flapping towards him out of the west, he saw, etched against the glassy sky, the form and outline of another dragon.

Oh dear, thought Reginald. *I do hope this doesn't mean trouble.* But trouble it undoubtedly was.

The dragon swooped round the valley once in a long extended circle and with a few flaps of his leathery wings alighted on the grass near Reginald. Instantly it burst into flames.

"Oh dear," murmured Reginald, feeling trouble or rather Trouble with a capital T growing nearer every moment. He squirmed like a naughty schoolboy about to be faced with a stern headmaster.

The dragon was larger than Reginald and had scales of burnished copper. Two sulphurous clouds of smoke rose thickly from his nostrils. His eyes were the colour of honey and his claws shone like polished brass.

"Reginald," he boomed, his voice rumbling like distant thunder.

"Yes?" said Reginald weakly. "How – uh – nice to see you again. When was the last time we met?" He fingered the daisy he was holding nervously.

"Do you know why I have come?" frowned the copper dragon majestically.

"No – not really," stammered Reginald. He shrugged his scaly shoulders and the row of fins on his long, sinuous back trembled.

"We're very disappointed with you – very!" said the copper dragon, getting down to business right away. His name was Bertram and in dragon circles he was extremely high-up and official. Reginald coiled up and looked glum. He shook his head appealingly and helplessly.

"You were given this portion of land to terrorize and you do nothing! Why, you're a laughing stock! No one in good dragon society would dare to receive you."

Reginald could not remember the last time he had bothered to approach good dragon society, but he kept his mountainous, jagged teeth clamped shut on his thick jewel-encrusted tongue and said nothing.

"When was the last time you terrorized a maiden?"

Reginald said nothing.

"When was the last time you rained down fire on a village?"

Reginald said nothing.

"It's hopeless! Hopeless! Don't you understand? We're in the business of control. Unless we keep the men down, think what will happen. If you don't burn the villages to the south the men will explore, advance, choke and cut down the forest. If you don't terrorize a few maidens, those humans will grow cocky and think that they rule the roost. Is that what you want to happen?"

Reginald shook his head vigorously.

"No, of course not," continued Bertram. "You have an important job to do, a tradition to keep up. You ought to be proud of these things and not disgrace them. What would your father have said? I remember him in the old days – a hundred thousand knights extinguished in one gush of flame – now *that* was something to see." Bertram's honey eyes burned excitedly at the memory.

"But you," he rumbled accusingly, "if you don't buck up, you'll have your licence revoked and you know what that means!"

Reginald searched the cavern of his brain. It was big and did not contain much information. He wrinkled his snout. "Remind me," he said feebly.

"Your fire will be put out and you'll be condemned to lie on an ice floe near the North Pole for the rest of your life."

Reginald shuddered. He never could abide fish and seals and other creatures from the sea — slimy, furry things tasting of salt. "Ugh!" he said.

"Now," said Bertram, "I want to see your contract. Where is it?"

"My contract?" breathed Reginald. "It's in there, I think." He pointed with a curved claw at the squashed-circle mouth of his cave.

"Go and get it then," hissed Bertram impatiently. "Honestly, you haven't a clue. When robbers came to steal your treasure you didn't even wake up!"

"I was tired," said Reginald. "Besides, they didn't take much."

"As much as they could carry probably," growled Bertram. "Do you want people to laugh at dragons?" He said this as though the idea were more chilling than the ice floe Reginald might be condemned to lie on. Dragons are fairly humourless creatures, but then they have fairly humourless jobs.

Reginald lumbered into his cave, leaving only four feet of his pointed tail threshing about in the sunlight. There was a clink and a rumble and the crash of pots and pans and chalices and breastplates from the darkness within. Finally Reginald's snout reappeared, his eyes as wide and as round as dinner plates. In one claw he grasped a rolled, yellowed parchment tied up with a crimson ribbon.

"I found it," said Reginald cheerfully. "The place is a bit of a mess, though."

"Congratulations," said Bertram drily, taking the scroll from him. He unrolled it with one claw, pinning the parchment to the ground with the other. The parchment was written impressively in dragon runes painted on in the old style.

"You see," said Bertram.

"What?" said Reginald.

"It says here. Look."

Reginald squinted and twisted his long back.

"One," read Bertram, "I hereby undertake to fulfil my duties as a dragon in the region allotted to me. Two: I will terrorize maidens whenever possible. Three: I will guard what treasure I can amass jealously and loyally with loss of life and limb to anyone who may

try to steal it. Four: I will be fearsome and firesome at all time. Five . . ."

Bertram read on and on till he came to number twenty-nine. Twenty-nine! Bertram's voice marched relentlessly through all twenty-nine articles of the Dragon's Code and as he read Reginald sat looking away in shame, tapping his claws on the grass. He knew he had not kept one of them. Bertram knew he had not kept one. The trouble was, Reginald did not want to spend his time burning and terrorizing. Burning and terrorizing bored him to bits. But the thought of being chained to an ice floe resolved him to try – for a little while at least.

"What do you say to that then – eh?" grated Bertram. Small tongues of fire fringed his lips.

But there was nothing, nothing Reginald could say. He wished Bertram would spread his wings and flap off and leave him in peace.

"You have three months," warned Bertram. "And then I'll be back. If you haven't improved your performance by then there'll be a price to pay. They say it's cold up at the North Pole at this time of the year." Bertram smiled grimly, revealing two rows of sharp, diamond teeth. Spreading out his wide wings, he gave one, two, three flaps and lifted a few inches off the ground. "Mind what I say. The Dragon Council will be watching you from now on."

Reginald watched Bertram's bulk recede, with a mournful expression on his face, till Bertram was only a dot on the horizon.

What to do? What to do? thought Reginald anxiously. But after all that unpleasant excitement he really and most truly thought he deserved a rest.

"Later," he purred, squeezing into a comfortable position. "I'll think about it later." And he fell asleep.

For the first week after Bertram's visit Reginald did nothing but sleep and worry. He slept more than he worried, as he found sleep to be a good solution to the problems he faced when he was awake. He knew his weak resolution would not carry him far – it hardly carried him to the end of the valley. For a couple of days he tried scouting around. Once he tried blasting a tree, but he was so out of practice that he only singed its leaves and swallowed most of his own fire by mistake which made him feel quite ill. He was glad no one had caught sight of him making this blunder and fled the scene with embarrassment, leaving the barely smoking tree wondering what had happened to it.

His dread of the ice floe began to wane after this disaster. He played in his mind with the words Bertram had spoken to him, trying to take the sting out of them, and at last he managed to convince himself that the copper dragon probably had not meant what he had said. Reginald was one of those creatures who, being so safe and secure in their own little nests and leading such pleasant trouble-free lives, believe nothing bad can happen to them.

He received a rude jolt, however, when a letter from Bertram arrived:

Dear Reginald,

I hope you have taken my words to heart. The Council meets at the end of August to decide on your future. I shall be back to visit you sometime before then. Jonathan has won the maiden-terrorizing cup again this year for the third time running. Sickening, isn't it! I enclose a picture of an ice floe to remind you what will happen to you if you don't shake yourself up a bit.

Yours with best wishes,
Bertram.

"Oh, the beast," howled Reginald. "Ruining my life like this!" And he had a good half-hour's malice thinking of what he would like to do to Bertram. It must have been good exercise for him since, for the first time in years, he soared up into the sky and flapped off to where the villages of men had lain undisturbed for generations.

A little to the north, and a little to the west of where Reginald lived in his pleasant valley, there was a castle, and in this castle

lived Princess Rosie, a wilful king's daughter.
That is, *she* was wilful. The king, a man as
meek as a mole, preferred paperwork to
people. He had a chancellor who dealt with
his subjects and gave in to his daughter
wherever possible. He did, however, have
plans. Rosie was sixteen, too old for a nurse
and too young for a husband. She had
burning, spark-filled eyes, red flaming hair
and freckles. And a temper. What a temper!
That morning she had fairly screamed at her
nurse, "I am not a child! I am not!" thus
proving how much of a child she still was.
Against the nurse's orders, she rode away on
her pony Quartermaine – on her own. The
poor nurse wrung her hands and sobbed into
her rocking chair. Soon the garment she was
knitting was soaked right through and
dripped down on to the floor.

Rosie was really in a temper because
rumours had fluttered to her ears about her
father's plans for her. There lived, two seas
away from them, her uncle and aunt and
cousin. Her cousin was a pimply, gangly

youth called Prince Humphrey. As a child the prince had loved to climb trees and when he was very young had acquired the nickname "Squirrel" which had stuck. The rumour that the princess heard, whispered to her by her nurse who never could keep a secret, was that she was to be presented to Prince Squirrel as a possible bride. Bride! She had scarcely laid aside her hoop and skipping rope. Princess Rosie stewed in her anger for days, clutching her pillow over her face and squealing, "Never. Never. Never. Never will I marry that spotty pudding! He can't even ride a horse straight!"

So she had ridden away, over the river and through the meadow, taken a wrong turning, tumbled off her horse and found herself alone and lost. Lost! She rubbed her head. There was a painful bump rising gently under her fingers. It was all too much. Too much! She glanced around, still sprawled in the long grass. There was not one hoof-nail of Quartermaine to be seen.

When I get hold of that horse . . . she

thought angrily, twisting her hands together. But she knew, sadly, that she was where she was through her own fault. *I suppose I was riding him too hard – and not looking where I was going.*

It so happened that Reginald, still smouldering from Bertram's letter, was scouting around over the place where Rosie sat. He was looking for someone to terrorize. Anyone would do so long as they were not too big and strong. Tree-burning had not been a success so, scoring Article One off the list, he had decided to have a go at Article Two and go back to Article One later on when he felt more capable. Dragons are keen-eyed and Reginald spotted Rosie's riding breeches from high up in the air. He was so high up he seemed to her only the outline of a distant bird.

Aha! thought Reginald to himself. *Prey! Oh – goody! Now, is she quite alone?* He checked, and to his satisfaction saw there was no other human being near her.

"Foolish girl," he mumbled and, pointing

his snout earthwards, turned his body into a dive. Rosie heard the struggle of wings in the air above her and, looking up, saw Reginald's glittering body snake its way down to the ground in front of her. The dragon reared up on his hind legs, rattled his wings, shook his podgy claws and roared. Rosie looked at him – well – rather as she would have done at her father if he had dressed up in a silly suit and done childish party tricks. Disdainful – yes. Amazed – yes. Disgusted – slightly. Afraid – no.

"What do you want?" she said, not turning a hair, for princesses rarely turn one in any situation. "I'm lost. Maybe you can help me find my way back."

"Eeargh – argh – harrgh – er!" roared Reginald, and he set fire to a hawthorn bush with two gobs of flame.

"Have you got something stuck in your throat?" asked Rosie a little concerned.

"Nnyeeargh – ghghgh – gh!" Reginald's eyes opened, his nostrils contracted and he roared, roared with all his might. The trees shook. The grass quivered . . . and . . . and . . . he dissolved into a fit of coughing that racked his massive stomach.

"It's no use," he said, "no use at all. You're not frightened, are you?" he complained disappointedly.

"No, not at all," returned Rosie. "Should I be?"

"Yes, yes, YES!" wailed Reginald, sprouting two feathers of white smoke out of his nostrils.

"Why didn't you say?"

"I'm not supposed to say. You're supposed to tremble naturally." Reginald was feeling quite offish. He could be huffy when he liked.

Rosie, looking at his ridiculous bulk and listening to his petulant voice, began to giggle. She made a little stuttering noise. Then her body shook. Then tears ran down her cheeks. Then she laughed out loud. Reginald ground his teeth together, sullen and hurt. "When you've quite finished," he interrupted, peeved. "I'm going to carry you off to my lair."

"Fine," said Rosie, equal to anything Reginald might say. "But don't drop me or I shall never forgive you."

Reginald picked up Rosie in his two claws and set her on his back. Her hands clasped the toughest of his pointed fins. It was the one nearest his neck. With one, two, three flaps of his wings, Reginald hovered a few inches off the ground and rose slowly above the trees. Beneath them the valley spread out in a patchwork shape: woods and fields and rivers. In a great arc, up above the tufts of combed-out cloud and down again, Reginald soared and fell. If on the earth he was cumbersome and heavy, in the air he was as light as a feather, as sleek as a dolphin and as graceful as a bird. He was as particular about his flying as a great pianist is about his playing. Reginald knew that flying was the one thing he was specially good at and he wanted to impress Rosie.

When they landed by the mouth of Reginald's cave Rosie was beaming, her cheeks glowing and her eyes shining. "That

was so good," she said. "You will take me up again, won't you?" She straightened her mouth into an appealing line.

Reginald despaired. For a terrorization this was not going well at all. He thought of holding her to ransom and swapping her for a few gold cups to build up his pile of treasure, but had to decide against this idea as kidnapping and ransom were not part of the dragon code of ethics. Reginald rubbed his claws together and pushed his snout into Rosie's face.

"Would you like some tea?" he asked.

"That would be lovely," said Rosie.

And they had a lovely afternoon together. That was the problem. As they munched buns and sticky cake, Reginald was haunted by thoughts of the ice floe waiting for him up at the North Pole. Both his ears drooped and he looked disgruntled.

"What's the matter?" asked Rosie, her mouth full of sticky cake.

Reginald heaved his shoulders and gave a sigh. Three sparks tumbled from his lips. Terrorization had been a failure. He told Rosie everything. He told her what a disgrace he was to dragonkind and about what the Dragon Council thought of him and about what he had to do for them and about what would happen to him if he didn't.

"You poor thing," sympathized Rosie. "How beastly. But bureaucrats are always the same. Daddy says so." And she told Reginald about how she had heard her father planned to marry her to Prince Humphrey and how she never would and how she had run away, fallen off her horse and found herself lost.

"A fine pair we are," she said, and gave a wry smile. "We can't seem to please anybody."

By the time they had finished talking to each other it was night. The air was like honey. The moon swam high in the sky. Reginald warmed some heather for Rosie to lie on and laid a blanket over her. He tucked his head under his tail, and with one dreamy snore was soon asleep.

In the morning Rosie was stiff but happy. "Morning," she called cheerily. Reginald lifted one heavy eyelid with difficulty. He was not an early riser at the best of times. "I expect they'll be looking for me everywhere," yawned the girl.

"I expect I should take you back," said Reginald.

"Oh, not yet," said Rosie. "I want another ride on your back."

And so the morning passed into afternoon, and they both enjoyed themselves so much that they forgot all about the time, until Reginald decided that he wanted his afternoon snooze. Rosie, who had had enough of afternoon snoozes as a child, left Reginald in his cave and went for a walk along the brook and up the hill. She climbed high above the valley. Neither she nor Reginald thought to worry about the thickening clouds above them. As she stood on the peak of the hill she suddenly felt a few drops of rainwater spatter on her cheek. *Oh dear,* she thought, and decided to turn back. The sky was a horrible grey-green colour and the valley below was breathless and still. As Rosie turned, there was a crash and a flicker of light. In an instant rain was driving into the ground like nails. Rosie was drenched. Drops of water tumbled over her face and down her neck. Harder it fell. The rain fell so hard it hurt. It was difficult to breathe. Rosie started to run. She ran down the hill, wild and unthinking, with the water streaming over her face. Down she ran till she stumbled and fell in the mud. She lay still.

Crash! There was a crash and a flicker of light. Reginald opened his right eye.

"Are you back, Rosie? Do try to make less noise!" Crash! The dragon sat bolt upright and knocked his head on the ceiling of his cave. Some broken rocks and dust fell on to the floor. "Rosie?" he asked worriedly in the darkness. "Rosie?" But there was no answer. "Dear me," said Reginald. "Can she be out in this?" The dragon's saucer eyes blinked at the solid lines of grey rain outside and its noise, like the rush of a thousand knights, assaulted his ears.

"I suppose I shall have to go and look for her."

This was braver than it sounded, because although dragons are better protected than the strongest knight in his toughest armour, they ought not to go out in the rain as it quenches their fire. But Reginald, distressed and concerned for Rosie's safety, forgot about his own and without a moment's ado flew up into the rain. He could have flown above the rainclouds and kept dry, but then he would not have seen Rosie through the grey fleecy blanket. Instead, he let the rain ping like arrows on his scales as he scanned the valley from top to bottom.

Reginald wheeled and circled, flapped and flew, till finally he saw the body of the girl lying half in water, half in mud on the side of the hill. Gently he picked her up in his mouth. Her head hung down. Her arms dangled limply. But Reginald knew she was alive because he could feel her heart beating. He knew too that her heart was like a drum, beating the end of his miserable career as a dragon.

Back in the cave he laid her carefully down, warmed her till she was dry, and fed her two spoonfuls of brandy. He sat by her for hours. He sat through that night and most of the next morning, until her eyelashes quivered and her eyes opened.

"Hello," she said weakly, "I've been having the most wonderful dream," and her face broke into a smile. Slowly, she sat up, and brushed one hand through her red hair. "But look at you!" she burst out.

Reginald felt rusty, squeaky and pathetic. His scales were dull and his snout shrivelled. Worst of all, his fire had gone out. There were no sparks left in his heart to kindle a flame. For the first time in his life he was cold and shaking.

"My fire has gone out," he croaked. If he could have cried he possibly would have then.

Rosie touched Reginald's snout with the end of her fingers. "You saved me," she said. "And you let that terrible thing happen to you. Love can't always help, but sometimes it is enough," and she breathed her warm, scented breath into the dragon's nostrils.

By some miracle Reginald's heart jumped and spluttered, and flames, real flames fanned by his own breath, burned up within him. He looked on in wonder as two trickles of smoke crawled out of his nostrils. He laughed, and by mistake singed one side of Rosie's hair. She let out a chuckle and shook her head. Reginald's fire was hotter than it had ever been before. For a moment he was ecstatic and whirled round his cave with delight, then soberly he whispered, "But the Council are only going to put it out again!"

"Not if we can help it," said Rosie and she began to tell Reginald the plans she had dreamed when she had been asleep.

The following afternoon found Reginald sailing through the sky like a galleon, his snout pointing in the direction of Rosie's father's castle. When he arrived at the castle battlements, he let out a dreadful shrieking and wailing and flew round and round the granite towers till the soldiers watching him felt sick and dizzy. Then, with remarkable dignity, Reginald descended to plant himself in the castle courtyard and roared, "Send me the king!"

The king appeared with a chalk face, quivering.

"Miserable man! I have your daughter!"

Rosie's face appeared from under one of Reginald's wings. "Oh, Daddy, Daddy! He can do the most dreadful things!"

"Silence!" ordered Reginald imperiously.

"Thirteen of your finest gold cups and shields, please!"

The king snapped his fingers and the soldiers stumbled over themselves in their haste to obey. The treasure was laid glinting in front of Reginald. The poor king was sweating hard.

"You can have your daughter back on one condition."

"Oh, anything!" pleaded the king.

"She must marry whom I say and whom I choose."

The king nodded nervously.

"You will see her later. Now, go!" Reginald roared most impressively and the king and his soldiers backed away. Reginald picked up the gold treasure in his claws and climbed into the air, shrieking all over the villages as he went.

"Do you think it worked?" he asked Rosie anxiously when they were up above the clouds.

"You were superb," she said.

Back at the cave the two of them heaped up

the new treasure on Reginald's existing meagre pile. "Did Daddy give you this?" said Rosie. "He never liked it. It was a present from Granny. Still – it *is* gold, I suppose. There: that looks most impressive. Now you must . . ."

"Must I?"

"Yes, it's bound to fool them."

A little sadly, Reginald sharpened one of his claws and cut off most of Rosie's hair. He laid it by a pile of blackened sheep bones.

"Just say she was any maiden," suggested Rosie. "They'll probably be so thrilled you've killed someone that they won't look too closely. Now . . . take me back – and we'll both face the music. Good luck!"

Reginald left Rosie outside her father's castle door. Of course, there had been a panic when it was found out she was missing, and then when the dragon appeared . . .

Rosie bore all the tears and the pampering well enough, only glad she had escaped from Prince Humphrey. Her father had already despatched a letter cancelling all the arrangements for her to go to see the pimply boy and he was so happy to have his daughter back that he forgot completely about marriage for a long time.

Reginald spent a couple of days blasting rocks to make the area around his cave as desolate and dragon-inhabited as possible. When Bertram finally swooped in, he was obviously surprised. His copper scales rustled with disbelief.

Reginald showed him the pile of treasure, the bones and the hair, and told him that he had managed to terrify a king and a few villages.

"Well, it's a start," said Bertram grudgingly. "I hope you'll go on improving from now on. You've had a lucky escape." Reginald wagged his head in agreement. Only he knew how lucky.

"I'll be back," said Bertram. "And I'll put in a good word for you at the Council."

"Thanks!" shouted Reginald, but Bertram was gone.

Reginald vanished soon after that. His cave was found empty by Bertram on one of his return visits. The treasure was gone. After a few years Reginald's name was removed from the list of official dragons and his own kind forgot him.

Rosie ruled her kingdom well after her father died and married late in life. There was a legend told about her that when the moon was full she could be seen soaring through the sky on the back of a fiery dragon, but like most legends, no one knew whether it was true or not. Rosie only winked when people asked her about it and pretended not to know what they were talking about.

A Good Sixpenn'orth

Bill Naughton

Three of us were on our way home from school one January afternoon when a man with a cigarette end in his mouth asked us would we like a job. "I want you to cart this loose load of coal into that coal shed. It'll be worth a bob," he added.

"Apiece?" I asked.

"Between you," he said.

It was an enormous heap of large coal gleaming in the grey light of the back street. We gazed at it for a minute, and then had a whisper among us. "Make it eighteen pence, mister," I suggested, "an' we'll take it on – for then we'll have a tanner each."

He agreed, and we set to work. Harry Finch

filled the buckets, I ran in with them, and Basher stacked it inside the shed. The man leant on a broom and flicked an occasional piece of coal from my path. He kept blowing on his hands to keep warm. Two hours saw the job done, by which time the sweat was pouring out of us, and I was feeling weak in the legs. Then the man knocked on the back door, and a woman came out and gave him half a crown. He turned and gave us sixpence each.

"Not much," I said, looking at the little coin in my blistered hand, "considering you got a bob."

"I'm the contractor," he said. "And don't forget, you'd have had nothing but for me."

"He's right," agreed Harry and Basher. "And besides," went on Harry, "just think of the fun we can have with a tanner at the Fair. The new year rush is over, and all the prices are down, because it travels tomorrow."

"Good idea," I said. "I'll meet you at seven o'clock, an' we'll go to the Fair and have a right good tanner's worth."

Scrubbed and excited, the three of us met on time and made off for the Fair. Once clear of the narrow streets and high black factories, we spotted from the main road the strange pale glow like a halo over the Fair. We walked faster, and as we neared the fairground we were caught by the exciting smells, fragments of blaring music and voices, and by the sense of movement: of roundabouts, big swings, cakewalks, helter-skelters, and whatnot, so that we broke into a trot.

The ground under our feet was slushy, and the glaring lights illuminated an almost deserted Fair. We liked it that way. Our heads stopped reeling, and we were able to stroll about the place and savour the atmosphere without being overcome and spending our money rashly.

"Take it easy," I warned my mates, "and let's keep scouting around till we've found the top value for money."

We watched the Flying Pigs, Big Boats, Bumper Cars, all going cheap, but we clung to our sixpences. We inspected every game of chance and skill: Hoopla, All Press, Dartboards, Ringboards, Roll-a-Penny, Skittles, Bagatelle, Rifle Range, and Coconut Shies.

"Look at that hairy 'un," whispered Harry. "I've allus wanted to knock off a coconut – and I reckon that 'ud drop with a touch."

"That's what you think," I said.

"I vote we have a good feed of them hot peas," said Basher. "Just smell 'um. What you spend on your guts, my mum reckons, is never lost."

"Don't rush it, Basher," I said.

"A coconut's the best bet," said Harry. "You might even knock *two* off – and they'd last for days."

"We didn't come by our money so easy," I cautioned them, "so let's use our discretion afore we part with it."

At that moment my eye caught sight of the figure of a man in silk shirt and riding breeches, a silver-handled whip in his hand, poised on a platform beneath the brightest lights on the fairground.

"Ladies and gentlemen," called out a beautiful blond lady. "Introducing Waldo – the greatest lion tamer of all time. Any moment now he will enter the cage of Nero! Nero the Untameable! The African jungle lion that has killed four trainers – the largest lion in Europe – the fiercest in captivity. Waldo will positively enter his cage! Will he come out alive?"

I felt hands tugging me back by the jacket. "Hy, where are you off?" asked Basher.

"Quick," I said, "let's get in afore the crowd."

"What crowd?" asked Harry.

"One small coin, ladies and gentlemen, sixpence only, brings you the greatest thrill of all time!"

"Keep still," hissed Basher.

"Get your tanners ready," I said, "we can't afford to miss it."

"No, you don't," said Basher. "Black peas, a whacking great plateful for tuppence, an' finish off with roasted spuds."

"Big hairy coconuts," whispered Harry.

I couldn't take my eyes off Waldo, unsmiling and unafraid. He bowed to us, stepped from the platform, and disappeared. Before Basher and Harry could hold me I was at the paybox.

"Half, please."

"*Half*? Why, you're getting in for a *quarter* tonight. Two bob's the proper price . . . You don't expect to see a chap eaten by a lion for threepence?"

I handed over the sixpence. I waved to my mates, but they wouldn't come. So I quickly went inside the tent, so as to get near the front. Inside were four people, and they looked at me pityingly. There was a well-dressed couple, an old man, and a woman who looked like a Sunday school teacher. It was very cold, and after the bright lights outside one could only see dimly. I went and stood near the stage.

There was no sign of Waldo. After a long time I heard the beating of a drum and the woman announcer. I felt like going out again and listening.

"We can't wait much longer," I heard the

man say to the woman. "Is he never going to go in to that wretched beast?"

Only five more people came in during the next twenty minutes. I felt chilled, and I was aware of an empty spot of skin in the palm of my hand, where I had clutched the sixpence. Then there was a final beating of the drum, and Waldo appeared on the stage before me.

His face was all powdered, and there was a smell of stale beer off him. He looked at us with disgust. And then the announcer bustled in. The curtain was pulled open, and there was a cage. Lying in the nearest corner was a big lion. It was less than a yard away from me, and it blinked its eyes and gave a good-tempered yawn.

"During the act, ladies and gentlemen, there must be complete silence. One sound, and Waldo may never come out alive. His life is in your hands. Since no insurance company will insure Waldo's life, I ask any of you who can afford it to place an extra coin in the hat. Thank you!"

Waldo cracked his whip outside the cage,

and Nero slowly got to its feet. The woman took a revolver out of her pocket. Waldo went to the door of the cage, and sprang back when the lion came. This seemed to disturb the lion. As it moved away Waldo quickly opened the cage and darted inside. He cracked the whip, and Nero loped wearily round the cage. He went after it, cracking the whip over his head. "*Silence!*" called the announcer. Nero skipped round the cage for about two minutes, then sank down to rest in the same corner. Waldo leapt to the door, opened it, and got out. Nero never moved. It looked at me again, blinked, sighed, and rested.

"Ladies and gentlemen," called the blond announcer, putting away the revolver, "that concludes the performance."

I couldn't believe it.

I exchanged one last look with the lion as the curtain was drawn across the stage. I even clapped feebly with the others. And the next thing I was outside.

"Look!" shouted Harry Finch. "That shaggy 'un – I knocked it off." He dangled an

enormous coconut before my eyes.

"Black peas an' roasted spuds," sighed
Basher. "Here" – he grabbed my head and
pressed my ear against his fat, warm stomach
– "can you hear 'em churning about inside?
Luv'ly."

Harry shook the coconut against my ear.
"Fair loaded with milk. I knocked it clean off
with the last ball. A right good tanner's
worth."

"Not as good as mine," said Basher. "First I

had a plate of hot peas, then a bag of roasted spuds, an' then another plate of hot peas."

The image of old Nero seemed fastened before my eyes; the smell of the lion, the sleepy old head, and gentle blinking eyes. *The fiercest lion in captivity*. We went walking along the streets homeward.

"How was the lion-taming show?" they asked at last.

"Champion," I said. "Worth anybody's money."

"You've not had much to say about it," remarked Harry suspiciously.

"Yes, you've kept your trap shut," accused Basher.

"It were that exciting," I said, "as it took my breath away."

"Something did," they said.

I longed to tell them, to unload the misery of my heart, but I dared not. I'd never have lived it down if I had.

"Sorry, lads," I said, "but I've got to be in early." And I ran off home.

*

I slept badly that night. Next morning when I was on my way to school Harry Finch called out, "He's here, Mum!"

"What's up?" I asked.

"Haven't you heard?" he said.

"Heard what?" I said.

"Waldo the Lion Tamer has been badly mauled by that wild lion. It's on the front page of the *Dispatch*. I told me mum an' she wants to ask you about it."

Out came Mrs Finch with her spectacles on and the *Dispatch* in her hand. "Ee luv, they say he's in a critical condition—"

"Let's have a look, please," I said to Mrs Finch. It was true. The lion had mauled him! I gave her the paper back. "I'm not surprised," I said, "the way that lion went at him. It clawed the blinking shirt off his back. He could hardly hold it at bay with his whip, an' a woman with a revolver was about to shoot it."

"Ee, suffering Simon! An' did you see all that?"

"'Course I did. Your Harry had a coconut instead."

By this time a few neighbours were at their doors, and when I went off there was a crowd of lads all wanting to hear about Waldo and Nero. I described the powerful physique of Waldo, and the beauty of the woman with the revolver, and told of the wild roaring lion that tried to claw at me through the bars. The school whistle made us run, but in the classroom they began to whisper questions to me. Teacher told me to stop talking.

"Please, miss," said Harry, "it isn't his fault. He was telling me about seeing Waldo the Lion Tamer all but torn to bits last night."

"Is that the person who was so severely mauled?" she asked. "Then you'd better come in front and tell us all."

I went to the front of the classroom and began. "The lion was making furious deep-throated roars even before Waldo attempted to get into the cage. And when it caught sight of him in his blue silk shirt it went into a fury. I was very close to the cage, and when its huge body hit the bars it made the whole tent shudder. The roars were blood-curdling."

Suddenly the class door opened and in came Mr Victor, the Headmaster. I was going back to my place, but he called me out again. "Oh, I must hear this – please continue."

I began all over again, adding any new bits that came to mind, when suddenly there was a knock on the door and a monitor ushered in Major Platt, the Inspector of Schools.

"I'm afraid I've interrupted something," he said.

"Not at all, Major," said Mr Victor hurriedly. "It just happens that this boy was present at the fairground performance last evening when the lion tamer was so badly mauled."

"My goodness, I must hear this!" exclaimed Major Platt. All three of them sat down, and I stepped back a foot to stand on the teacher's platform. I felt in fine form.

"After three attempts to enter the cage the lady with the pearl-handled revolver tried to dissuade the Great Waldo, but he refused to give up, and I heard him say: 'The show must go on.' Then, by a ruse, he got Nero away from the door, and the next moment he was inside. The iron door slammed after him. He was alone in the cage with the African man-eating lion. A mighty roar rended the air at that moment, and the big crowd shuddered. Waldo attempted bravely to keep the lion down with his whip – but it gave one spring. The next moment I saw his silk shirt fall to shreds on the floor. But he was unhurt. He drove it into a corner – again it sprang. The woman darted to the bars with the revolver, but I heard Waldo shout, 'Don't shoot!' His eye never left that of the lion. For a long time it parried, trying to knock the whip from his hand. Then at last it succeeded, and again it sprang with an angry roar. Waldo fell to the floor. But in a trice he was clear. But he couldn't get to the door of the cage. And he had lost his whip. The lion seemed to be sizing him up. Then, just as it was about to spring, he snatched a piece of shirt from the floor and waved it in front of its face. When it sprang he was already at the door. The blond lady unfastened it. Just in the nick of time he got out. Then I noticed a line of blood across his bare back. The entire place trembled as the lion hit the door. Waldo could scarcely stand up. I was right up in front of the crowd. He gave a bow to the audience, and then the lady helped him away. The audience clapped like mad. The lion snarled with fury. Then I went out to meet my mates. One was eating hot peas. The other had knocked off a hairy coconut."

Major Platt, smiling solemnly, or so it seemed to me, patted me on the head. "One day, my boy," he said, "you will make a true journalist." And he slipped a thick, heavy coin into my fist.

Modestly I went back to my place between Harry and Basher. Their eyes were fastened enviously on me, and I couldn't resist opening my hand and letting them glimpse the half-crown. They let out a gasp. And Harry grunted, "The lion turned out the best sixpenn'orth after all."

As I sat down I felt the excitement drain away, and Harry's words brought up a picture of the real Nero before me. I saw the two old eyes of Nero, so weary and worn, and I wondered at the agony it must have suffered to provoke its old jungle temper. In fact, I had half a mind to go out and confess the truth before the entire class. I felt that was the right thing to do. And I would have done it – only, I was a bit scared Major Platt might have taken the half-crown back.

Particle Goes Green

Helen Cresswell

Particle – more formally known as Richard Benson – is the nine-year-old son of two remarkable parents. His father, Bill, is a brilliant scientist and inventor who fills their house with gadgets; his mother, Fay, is a flamboyant actress. Particle and his sister Eve can never quite work out which parent they are like. But one thing is certain – there's never a dull moment in the Benson house!

Particle's witchcraft book arrived two days before the Bensons were due to go on holiday. Eve was always the first to the door when the postman came because she was expecting any day to hear that she had won a cabin cruiser in a competition she had entered.

"What's this?" she pondered, examining the parcel. It bore a Sussex postmark. "'Richard Benson, Esq.' – oh, it's that blessed Particle again. Now what?"

She took the book up to her younger brother's bedroom. She had to pick her way over brilliantly splashed sheets of newspaper where he had been action-painting the night before.

"Come on, Particle," she said. "Wake up."

He might, of course, already be awake. It was difficult to see through the mosquito net. He had been sleeping under it for three weeks now, despite the fact that Number 14 Sanders Close rarely saw a bluebottle, let alone a mosquito.

"I am awake," came his voice. "Has the post come?"

Eve pulled aside the net. Particle, already wearing his spectacles, was sitting up in bed making clothes-pegs. He had met a gypsy a few days before, camping in a field beyond the town. Particle had presented him with one of Bill's sports jackets, and in return the gypsy had shown him how to make clothes-pegs.

"Really, Particle! Look at all those shavings!"

"I've made fourteen since I woke up," Particle informed her, in his high, serious voice. "It's just a question of practice. That, and a bit of knack thrown in. I don't expect I shall ever be quite up to gypsy standard. Peg-making's inborn in them, over generations."

Eve, despite herself, regarded him fondly.

"He's so refreshing," she was always telling her friends. "Honestly, when you think what nine-year-old boys can be like . . . I mean, he's just like a dear little old man, sometimes."

"Is that for me?" inquired Particle. "The parcel?"

She handed it over. He gave a couple of expert twists with his jackknife and the book was in his hands.

"I shan't get up this morning," he told her. "I shall stay in bed and read this."

"What on earth is it? It's not even a new one. It's years old, if you ask me. How much did you pay for it?"

"*Binding Spells*." He held the book up.

"Binding what?"

"Spells."

"I've never heard of it. Who by?"

"A witch, I expect," he said. He turned the flyleaf. "Look at this – f's instead of s's! It's old, all right!" He was gleeful. "By Allifon Grofs. The Witch of Northumberland."

"Oh, Particle. You really are the limit. What on earth possessed you to send for that? And where's it from?"

"An antiquarian bookseller. I wrote to him. I asked him for a book on the subject of witchcraft of the greatest possible antiquity. This is it."

"How much?" asked Eve. "We're going on holiday the day after tomorrow, you know. You needn't come borrowing from me if you run out of money halfway through."

Particle shook the book and a letter fell out. He read it.

"Not all that expensive," he told her. "Not considering its antiquity."

"Well, I should get up, if I were you," Eve said. "Bill and Fay aren't going to like this a bit. In fact I expect you've done it on purpose, just to annoy them."

"Not at all," said Particle. He really did look like a little old man, propped up against his pillows in his too-large pyjamas and too-large spectacles. "They should both be very pleased. Witchcraft is an art and a science."

"I just hope so, that's all," Eve threw over her shoulder as she went. She paused by her parents' bedroom door. She could hear Bill's voice – they were evidently awake.

"Want a cup of tea?" she called. "Postman's been."

"Oh, bless you, darling," came Fay's voice, and the door opened. Eve kissed her mother and handed her the three letters.

"Nothing for you, dear?"

Eve shook her head.

"Never mind. You know what these competitions are. I'm sure you'll hear soon.

That marvellous slogan! I'll be down myself in a minute. I told Bill he could have a lie-in this morning while I scurry round packing and things."

Eve nodded and went on down. It was a morning just like any other morning. Even the book on witchcraft didn't mark it as anything special – not at the time. The sunlight fell in pools on the golden oak floor and lit the copper bowl of roses on the chest.

Stepping into the kitchen first thing in the morning was always something of a jolt. It was not really so much a kitchen, Eve thought for the thousandth time, as a laboratory. Apart from that, it came as such a shock after the rest of the house. Whenever people remarked on it, Fay always said:

"Ah, well, of course, the kitchen's Bill's. The rest of the house is pure me, but I gave him a free rein in the kitchen. After all, a kitchen's one place where you must be scientific, mustn't you?"

She would make one of her lovely vague gestures, press a knob and watch a tin opener glide from a concealed socket in the wall, or a waste disposal bin rise from the tiles. The guests would crowd in, enchanted, and Fay would run through the whole performance, igniting cookers, boiling water, making mayonnaise, all by remote control. As her final piece she would always get them to look through the window and then close the front gates under their very eyes. Back in the drawing room with its oak beams, inglenook and Dresden china, the guests would wonder if they had dreamed it all.

"I'm so thankful I married a scientist," Fay would coo, drifting in with a tray of sandwiches that had been cut, buttered and filled by Bill's latest recruit to the army of kitchen robots. "It's so relaxing."

Eve herself was never so sure. Bill and Fay were both marvellous in their own ways, she appreciated that. It was just that sometimes she felt as if her own personality were being split in two by them, and she herself was a strange hybrid of half-scientist, half-actress. It was so confusing.

Even Particle seemed to suffer from it. The ideas he had, all the outrageous schemes, were straight from Fay. But the precision, the deadly earnestness with which he pursued each one to its logical (or even illogical) conclusion, was unmistakably the same as the passion that drove Bill to pursue electrons into the early hours of the morning, and invent devices so secret that they had to install a concealed safe behind the nineteenth-century print of skaters in the dining room.

Not that Bill was usually anxious to claim Particle as his own. From the time when Particle had begun to have ideas of his own and put them forward in his high, reedy voice, Bill had been frowning and cross-questioning and finally exploding.

"There isn't a particle of sense in a word you're saying! Not a particle!"

Eve sighed as she regulated the dial for the toast. The holiday began tomorrow – in fact it had as good as started already, since Bill was staying at home – and holidays always seemed to point the problem more sharply. *One of these days*, she thought, *I really shall have to make my mind up. Which am I? Bill or Fay?* It occurred to her that even the reason why she and Particle called their parents by their Christian names was not clear-cut. Bill believed in it because he thought that "Mummy" and "Daddy" were unscientific, sentimental and probably unhygienic. Fay simply thought that it was more modern and rather fun.

When Fay flounced in now, wearing one of her frilled housecoats and the lipstick without which she vowed she couldn't face the milkman, Eve wondered whether it might not be wise to mention the book on witchcraft. She realized that it was bound to produce one of the situations in which the cleft between science and art in the family would yawn into one of its periodic chasms. Fay was already producing from the wall the gadget that was to make her fresh lemon juice. Then the telephone rang and Fay cried:

"Heavens, the phone!" and made a swirling exit.

Eve arranged the neat, popped-up toast, ready-curled butter and home (machine) made marmalade on her father's tray. The egg (timed for three minutes, twenty seconds precisely) was placed in its stainless-steel heat-retaining eggcup with its bread (cut to three-eighths of an inch) and ready-spread butter (set at Number 3 – medium heavy spreading).

Satisfied, she picked up the tray, went to the door, trod on the door-operating switch and went into the hall where the newspapers, as if also operated by a timing device, were just appearing through the letter box.

Bill was already up, doing his three minutes' deep breathing by the window. Eve knew better than to interrupt. She laid the tray on the bedside table, blew a kiss towards his intent, reddened face and withdrew. She went back to Particle's room. He was still in bed.

"Come on," said Eve. "Get up. Fay'll never let you stop in bed. There's too much to do."

From behind the mosquito net came a low,

muffled chant. Particle had not even heard her.

"Oh, for heaven's sake!" cried Eve. "You're not chanting spells, I hope!"

She pulled back the mosquito net. Particle was still propped against his pillows, the book resting on his knees. He broke off, startled. Eve stared at him. She stared so hard that she could feel herself staring, her eyes fixed and bulging. He blinked at her, struck by her expression.

"What's the matter?" he demanded. "Your eyes are all—"

Then she screamed. She heard herself, too. When the scream – a long, high, frantic one – was out, she ran.

She collided with Fay in the hall.

"Eve! Whatever—"

Eve faced her mother. For a moment she was speechless. What she had to say was, after all, impossible. It must be.

"That scream. And you're white as a ghost. Whatever is it, darling?"

"It's Particle," Eve heard herself saying. "He's gone green."

Fay gasped. "Oh, Eve! Not one of his bilious attacks! Not at a time like this. He can't, he just can't!"

"You don't understand," cried Eve. "He's gone green actually!"

"I know it does sometimes seem like it," agreed Fay. "You'd better take him up some of his usual mixture, and if he stays in bed—"

"Green! Green!" Eve's voice was rising to a scream again.

"I'll go and have a look," said Fay. Eve, watching her go up the stairs, had a sudden wild hope that in a moment she would be down again, rummaging round for Particle's tummy mixture and grumbling all the while under her breath, and everything would be miraculously all right again.

Fay's scream was even louder than Eve's. Even Bill heard it – or perhaps by now he had finished his deep breathing anyway. Eve ran up the stairs to find them locked in collision by Particle's door.

"Green!" moaned Fay. "Oh Bill, I must be going mad!"

"Green!" repeated Bill. "What's green? Now come along, Fay, pull yourself together. And what's all this screaming?"

"Particle's green!" shrieked Fay. She stepped back and pointed a dramatic finger. "Look! Go on! Look!"

Bill went into the bedroom. Eve and Fay stared at each other, waiting. Bill came out.

"He is green," he admitted.

"Pea green!" shrieked Fay. "Do something, Bill!"

In the silence that followed, Eve was aware of the patter of light footsteps over the bedroom carpet, and for the first time thought of Particle, alone in there, green as grass and probably scared half out of his wits. She pushed past her parents and ran in to find him settling himself against the pillows and pulling up the blankets. His eyes behind the too-large spectacles looked enormous and she fancied that the green was a shade paler now – on his face, at least.

"Oh, Particle," she said, "what have you done?"

"I got up," he said in his high voice, "and had a look in the mirror . . . I think I had better stay in bed, after all."

He looked down at his hands, just visible below the cuffs of his tangerine pyjamas. They clashed horribly. Despite herself, Eve could not help noticing with interest that the actual fingernails were still pinkish. Particle,

116

too, was studying them intently, frowning a little.

"Is it – I mean – are you – all over?" asked Eve in a lowered voice.

Without speaking Particle drew a leg from under the bedclothes and waved a skinny, dragonish foot in the air. Eve let out another little scream and Particle looked at her reproachfully.

"I'm sorry, Particle," she said. "It's just the shock, you know."

Particle put his leg back under the blankets. As he did so, the book on witchcraft slid to the floor. Eve seized it.

"It's this!" she cried. "Isn't it? It's a spell!"

Particle nodded slowly.

"It must be," he said.

"Which one? Which?" Eve began to thumb feverishly through the pages. She seemed to remember that in all the fairy tales every spell had had an anti-spell, to undo it. That was usually where the good fairy had come in.

"It's no good doing that, you know," Particle told her. She looked up.

117

"Why not?"

"This is just volume 1, Spells and Charms," he said. "You need Volume 2 to lift them."

Eve dropped the book onto the bed. She looked again at Particle with his rumpled hair and calm, perfectly green face and had a sudden wild desire to burst into laughter. Downstairs she could hear the milk bottles being clattered onto the step, and beyond that her parents' high, excited voices. Hearing them reminded her. They did not know about the witchcraft. She made for the door, then turned.

"Wait here," she ordered. "Don't move. And don't dare read one other single spell. Don't dare!"

Fay was on the telephone. Eve opened her mouth but Bill held up a warning finger.

"Doctor!" he whispered loudly.

"No . . . no . . ." Fay was saying. "I mean really green, doctor. Yes . . . yes . . . he's got plenty of the medicine you gave him last time. No . . . yes . . . but Doctor, I mean actually green. Green!"

Her voice was rising to a shriek again. There was a small pause. "Yes, yes . . ." Her voice trailed off. She put the receiver down.

Eve and Bill looked enquiringly at her.

"He says he'll call tomorrow morning if he's no better," she said blankly. "Tomorrow! Oh, Bill! My poor little Particle!"

Bill looked definitely worried.

"Must be some bug or other," he said. "Has he got a temperature?"

"How do I know if he's got a temperature?" wailed Fay.

"We'll find out," said Bill. "Yes, that's the first thing. It should give us a pointer."

"I've heard of yellow fever," moaned Fay, "but this is green! There's no such thing! There's yellow fever and scarlet fever and I'm not sure there isn't a black fever, but I've never in all my life—"

"Now listen," said Bill, "you go and make some strong black coffee. There's some perfectly logical explanation for all this, and we'll find it in no time. Some kind of disturbance in pigmentation, perhaps, or

119

faulty diet, or – I'll go and get that thermometer."

He went out. Eve could see that now he was more interested than worried. He was going to do some research. Just as if poor little Particle were some specimen in a bottle, she thought disgustedly. To Fay she said:

"He needn't bother. There's nothing the matter with Particle – not in that way. It's a spell."

Fay looked at her. She seemed not to have heard.

"Catching . . ." she murmured. "What if it's catching?"

"It's witchcraft," Eve went on. "Particle sent for a book about it. It came this morning. When I went up just now he was chanting one of the spells. He must have picked the wrong one, or got it mixed up, or something, and—"

She broke off at the expression on Fay's face.

"Witchcraft?" Fay whispered. "Did you say witchcraft?"

Her face was an alarming, chalky white. It

occurred fleetingly to Eve that she didn't seem astonished or even surprised, simply . . . stunned.

"The witch of Northumberland, or something," said Eve. Bill came back with the thermometer.

"Normal," he said. "Not even a point in it. The little chap seems to be taking it all quite calmly. 'There's bound to be a remedy,' he says, cool as a cucumber. Quite scientific about the whole thing. A chip off the old block, after all."

Eve saw her mother's face change from white to red in an instant.

"Nonsense!" she said sharply.

Bill stared at her.

"All right," he said, "no need to be huffy. I merely said that in his whole approach to the thing—"

"I know what you said," Fay said.

Bill cleared his throat.

"I'll run him down to the surgery," he said. "See what Jenkins has to say. No, on second thoughts – the hospital. They've got the equipment there, and so on. This'll be right outside Jenkins' experience."

"No," said Fay.

They looked at her.

"Leave him alone," she said.

"But we're going on holiday the day after tomorrow," exploded Bill. "You're not proposing to take a pea-green child to the Royal, I hope. There was enough fuss last year about his marine specimens floating round in the washbasins, and if they once see him—"

"He'll be all right by then," said Fay.

Bill snorted.

"You mean you hope he'll be all right. If only you could learn the elementary lesson of distinguishing between personal wishes and scientific facts, you'd—"

"He will," said Fay. She rarely let Bill finish a sentence.

"Fay, can I have my breakfast now?"

It was Particle, in his dressing gown and slippers, looking more than ever like a pantomime hobgoblin, and so obviously impossible among the chintzy chairs and sporting prints that all further discussion was suddenly pointless.

"Of course, darling!" Fay rushed over and hugged him, something she often did, and usually to his annoyance, but this morning he seemed grateful, and even patted a thin green hand on her arm in return.

"Come and have it in the kitchen. Luckily it isn't one of Mrs D's days for coming in—" She broke off. "Oh I'm sorry, darling!"

"It's all right," said Particle. "I don't blame you. I do look pretty horrible green."

"Oh, you don't!" cried Fay, struck with remorse. "Does he, Eve? You look absolutely sweet, once the first shock of it wears off. Rather like a dear little . . . dear little . . . well, sweet anyway. It's just that Mrs D's such a dreadful gossip, and you can't possibly expect her to understand a thing like this. Now you—"

The door of the kitchen slid across and cut off her voice. Eve looked at Bill. He did not seem anxious to meet her eyes.

"Bound to be some scientific explanation," he said.

"Not this time," said Eve. It was out at last.

"What do you mean?"

"I mean," she said, "that Particle's gone green because there's a spell on him. It's witchcraft."

Bill stared at her for a moment, then roared with laughter. Eve watched him. Gradually his laughter tailed off rather uneasily under her serious gaze.

"That's rich, that is," he said.

"Yes, it is," agreed Eve. "I thought you'd see the funny side of it."

"What on earth gave you that idea, anyway?" Bill asked. "Lord, I've just remembered. My breakfast! I haven't touched it."

"It's in your room," Eve told him. "And if I were you, I should just take a look at that book on Particle's bed."

He looked startled, nodded, and went upstairs. Eve settled down to make a list for packing. After a while she became fidgety.

Fay and Particle were still in the kitchen. It was not long before she began to wonder if she had imagined the whole thing. Out of sight, a green Particle was even more impossible than when he was actually visible. Eve began to feel that she must have another look, or burst.

She went in. There was no doubt about it. Particle, green as ever, was eating his cornflakes while Fay was fiddling with the toaster. From the way they both looked at her Eve felt certain that they had been in the middle of a very interesting conversation.

"We've decided that the most sensible thing to do it just carry on exactly as if nothing had happened," Fay began.

"Oh?" said Eve. She felt nettled by the indefinable atmosphere of conspiracy that excluded herself. "Particle's going for his swimming lesson at eleven as usual, is he? That'll be interesting."

"Almost exactly as if nothing had happened," Fay amended. "Obviously Particle's not going parading about outside, but there's nothing to stop the rest of us carrying on as normal. There's plenty for Particle to do about the house. There's all his packing, for a start."

"Will we be going, then?" Eve asked.

"Yes, we shall," said Fay firmly.

"But Bill said—"

"Never mind what Bill said. He's far to scientific to have the least inkling of what's happening. And while we're on the subject, Particle and I have decided that it would be best not to mention anything about witchcraft to your father."

"It's too late," said Eve. "I've already told him."

"What did he say?" gasped Fay.

"He laughed."

Her mother seemed relieved.

"I'll go up and have a word with him," she said.

Eve watched her go. All things considered, she seemed to be taking the whole thing very calmly. She turned her attention back to Particle. For someone who was a rich and unbecoming pea green from head to toe and with no immediate prospect of ever being anything else, he too seemed irritatingly unconcerned.

"You know, later on," he said, "do you think you could possibly take a colour photo of me? Just for the records?"

"Honestly, Particle," she cried. "Fancy thinking of a thing like that at a time like this!"

"If we don't," said Particle, "no one's ever going to believe us. In fact about ten years from now we shan't even believe it ourselves."

Eve shuddered.

"I certainly hope I've forgotten about it long before then," she told him. Then, rather unkindly, "If, of course, you're not still green."

She immediately regretted saying it, but he munched imperturbably and seemed not to have noticed.

"It's all my own fault, of course," he said.

"Of course it is," said Eve. "Who else's?"

"No, I mean for not believing. It said as

clear as anything that the spell was for turning people green. I just didn't believe it."

"I should think not!" cried Eve. "As if anyone believes in spells and things in this day and age."

She stopped abruptly. There, set square among the glittering host of electronic gadgets, was the indisputable work of witchcraft. Wherever she looked she could see faint greenish reflections of it in the aluminium and stainless steel. She shivered.

Bill and Fay came in.

"It's all settled," said Fay almost gaily. "No hospital and no fuss. Now what does everyone want for lunch?"

It was a queer sort of day all the same. It was not just the frenzied scuffles and panics every time the doorbell rang, not even the sight of Particle himself, more impossible-looking than ever in his faded blue jeans and T-shirt. It was an extraordinary feeling of unreality that intensified as the day went on.

Eve went shopping in the afternoon, and walking down the street felt an almost irresistible urge to greet everyone she met with:

"Have you heard? My brother's gone green! Green as grass from top to toe!"

By the time she reached home her head was aching with the effort of not telling.

Oddly enough the one who was taking it hardest was Bill. At lunchtime Fay and Particle were making silly jokes about his eating up all his greens, and Eve noticed that Bill was the only one who was not laughing. By teatime he was thoroughly on edge. He sat darting restless, miserable looks at the serenely emerald Particle, and finally burst out:

"Right! That's enough of this whole farce. Get your things on, Particle."

Particle, halfway through a slice of chocolate cake, blinked enquiringly.

"We're going to the hospital."

"No," said Fay.

"If you think I'm going to sit here and watch a son of mine suffering from some obscure and horrible disease without—"

"Nonsense," said Fay calmly. "There's not a thing the matter with him."

"Not a thing the what?" roared Bill. "Look at him! Just look! We all sit around drinking tea and passing the sugar as if green people grew on trees! I won't have it! I won't have my son that impossible colour. It's impossible! It's beyond all reason!"

They all looked at him.

"It's witchcraft," said Eve at last.

"Don't keep saying that!" shouted Bill. He lowered his voice. "I'm sorry. I don't mean to shout. But you must stop all this medieval mumbo-jumbo about witchcraft. We are in the twentieth century. We have electric light. The atom has been split. There is no such thing as witchcraft."

"I didn't believe it, either," said Particle.

Bill glared at him, breathing heavily.

"All right!" he said. "We'll see!"

He stormed out.

"Oh dear," said Fay. She turned over a cup, the hot tea ran onto Eve's leg, Eve screamed and in the ensuing commotion it was not surprising that no one heard the front door-bell ring, or Bill's voice as he spoke to the visitor. They had just settled themselves when the door opened and Bill came in, saying:

"If you'd just like to wait here a moment, Constable, I'll . . ." His voice tailed away.

There was an enormous, welling, blinding silence. Particle, his chocolate cake poised halfway to his lips, stared at the constable. The constable, his face a mixture of horror and disbelief, stared back. The silence went on and on. It took possession. *Isn't anyone going to say anything,* thought Eve. *Ever?*

The policeman gave his head a violent shake, as if to clear his brain or vision. It evidently worked, because he turned his gaze away from Particle and over the others as if looking for clues on their blank faces.

"Good evening, Constable," said Fay firmly. "Will you have some tea?"

He shook his head.

"No? Perhaps you'd like to sit down a moment while my husband . . . Was it your licence and insurance he wanted to see, dear?"

"I'll get them," said Bill and vanished.

The constable sat suddenly. Eve looked at him with interest. She had never actually seen a policeman, complete with helmet, sitting in a chair before.

"Won't you take your hat off?" enquired Fay. "Are you sure you won't have some tea? Particle, fetch another cup and saucer, will you, darling?"

She's taking it too far, thought Eve. *This is one thing she won't talk her way out of.*

Particle got up and obediently padded into

the kitchen. He was barefoot, as he usually was in the house. The policeman's eyes followed his dragonish feet. Slowly he got to his feet. He cleared his throat.

"That . . . er . . . boy . . ." He nodded towards the door.

"Particle?" cried Fay. "Oh, take no notice of him, Constable. He's always—"

"He's green," said the constable accusingly.

"Well, yes," admitted Fay. "But only temporarily. You see—"

"All over, from what I could see," he went on. "From head to foot."

"Here we are!" It was Bill. "All in order, I think you'll find."

The policeman took the documents, examined them with irritating slowness and handed them back.

"Quite in order, sir. Sorry to have troubled you, but it's all part—"

"I know. Quite so. Perhaps I can see you out, if there's nothing else . . . ?"

"There's just this other little matter that's arisen, sir." The constable stood his ground.

"I'd like to ask one or two questions, sir, if you don't mind. About the green child, sir."

"Well?" said Bill.

"Well," said the policeman. "What about it? I mean, why is the child green?"

"The child is green entirely by his own choice," said Bill. "He chooses to be green."

"Temporarily," put in Fay.

"I don't like it, sir," said the policeman flatly. He looked about the room. Eve could tell that he was already beginning to wonder if he was dreaming the whole thing, now that Particle had disappeared.

"As far as I know," said Bill, "there's no actual law about people being green. Is there?"

"Well, sir—"

"Or any other colour, as far as I know," went on Bill. "As far as I know, a citizen is entitled to adopt any colour he chooses, as long as in so doing he does not constitute a public nuisance. If, for instance, I were to turn bright blue and then go dancing in my bathing trunks on Waterloo Bridge, thereby creating a disturbance and bringing traffic to a halt, that, in my view, would constitute an offence. But as to going green, blue, ginger or buff in the privacy of one's own home, then that's a very different matter indeed, Constable."

It was at moments like these that Eve could see the advantages of having a scientific mind. The policeman looked distinctly shaken. Then he rallied.

"That's a matter that will have to be gone into, sir," he said stiffly.

Then Particle returned with the cup and saucer. He grinned, and the flash of white teeth in his green face set the law again into a helpless boggle. Once or twice he opened his mouth as if he were going to say something to Particle, but was uncertain how to go about it, never having addressed a green person before.

"Will you have some tea, Constable?" enquired Fay sweetly.

"I shall not stop, thank you, madam," said the policeman. He rose. "I'll get along back to the station and make my report."

"I should think the inspector will enjoy that," commented Bill.

"The inspector will doubtless be calling himself, sir," said the policeman. "And the NSPCC will have to be informed as well, I'm afraid."

"The NSP—" Bill stared. Then he and Fay broke into uncontrollable mirth.

"Oh dear!" gasped Fay, her eyes watering.

The constable, with a final outraged glare at their helplessly heaving shoulders, went out. Fay, wiping her eyes, hurried after him, but too late. The front door banged. The laughter stopped abruptly.

"That's done it," said Bill. "We shall have Particle's picture plastered over every colour supplement in England now."

"You don't really think he'll come back, do you?" gurgled Fay. "Oh, it was so comical. Did you—"

"Comical?" Bill was shouting again. "Don't you realize what's happened? Don't you care? And what about Particle? Are you mad? Yes, you are!"

"There's no need to shout," said Fay. "If you hadn't let him in without warning us first this would never have happened. And now we shall have to do something I didn't want to do at all. Come along, Particle."

"Oh, Fay," said Particle. "I've hardly got used to the idea yet. Just let me—"

"Come along," said Fay. He came. Bill and Eve were left staring after them.

"Now what?" muttered Bill. "I'll go and get the car out."

"What for?"

"To get Particle away. They'll probably take him away."

"But why? Particle's just the same as he's always been. He's just green, that's all. I think he's even beginning to enjoy it."

"So do I," said Bill grimly. "I'll get the car."

Then Fay and Particle came in. Particle was no longer green. The shock was stunning. He looked exactly the same as he always had and yet, for an instant, was a stranger. In that moment Eve felt a curious sense of flatness and disappointment. The vital touch of magic was gone. The room seemed to shrink and settle into itself again. Everything was back to normal. She shivered.

"And what happened?" enquired Bill finally.

"I took the spell away," said Fay. "I'm a witch myself, you know. Not a real witch, but descended from witches."

"Witch?" croaked Bill.

"I know you don't believe in them," Fay said, "and if you like we'll forget all about what's happened and not mention it again. I wouldn't have told you if it hadn't been for the policeman. You see all those spells were twenty-four-hour ones – all the Northumberland Witch's are. Particle would have been as right as rain in the morning."

Particle was over by the mirror examining his face as if looking for any stray patches of green that might have been left. When he turned away Eve could see that he, too, was disappointed.

"We never even took those colour photos," he said.

"You could try again, some time," said Eve.

"It's no good. Fay said that was a chance in a million. You're supposed to be a seventh child of a seventh child, and I'm only the second. Fay says that the law of heredity—"

"Ah!" Bill's face brightened. "Heredity. Now as I see it, what happened was this: Fay herself, being the seventh child of a—"

"Sixth," said Fay.

"Pardon?"

"Sixth child of a seventh child," said Fay. "I told you, I'm not a real witch any more than Particle is. We just have our moments."

She and Particle exchanged smug glances. Bill said, "I'm going to make more tea."

They all followed him into the kitchen.

"Aaah!" Bill let out a long breath and looked around him with relief. He was on home territory. He fiddled with his dials for a long time, grateful for something that he could understand.

"You know," he said then, "It's obvious now what happened today."

"Oh?" said Fay.

"Yes. Mass hysteria. It's a well-known phenomenon. You see, Eve, knowing that Particle had a book on witchcraft, subconsciously—"

The front doorbell rang.

"I think that this," said Fay, "will be the police. And the NSPCC. And the reporters."

Then Bill said, "I think Particle had better answer the door, don't you?"

The Bensons looked at each other with sudden glee. Eve thought fleetingly, *Particle said witchcraft was an art and a science*, and then they were all crowding into the hall to see the fun. Because tomorrow it was going to be difficult to believe that any of this had happened at all, and the day after, harder still . . .

A Question of Grammar

Richmal Crompton

It was raining. It had been raining all morning. William was intensely bored with his family.

"What can I do?" he demanded of his father for the tenth time.

"*Nothing*!" said his father fiercely from behind his newspaper.

William followed his mother into the kitchen.

"What can I do?" he said plaintively.

"Couldn't you just sit quietly?" suggested his mother.

"That's not *doin'* anything," William said.

"I *could* sit quietly all day," he went on aggressively, "if I wanted."

"But you never do."

"No, 'cause there wouldn't be any *sense* in it, would there?"

"Couldn't you read or draw or something?"

"No, that's lessons. That's not doin' anything!"

"I could teach you to knit if you like."

With one crushing glance William left her.

He went to the drawing room, where his sister Ethel was knitting a jumper and talking to a friend.

"And I heard her say to him—" she was saying. She broke off with the sigh of a patient martyr as William came in. He sat down and glared at her. She exchanged a glance of resigned exasperation with her friend.

"What are you doing, William?" said the friend sweetly.

"Nothin'," said William with a scowl.

"Shut the door after you when you go out, won't you, William?" said Ethel equally sweetly.

William at that insult rose with dignity and went to the door. At the door he turned.

"I wun't stay here now," he said with slow contempt. "Not even if . . . even if . . . even if . . ." he paused to consider the most remote contingency, "not even if you wanted me," he said at last emphatically.

He shut the door behind him and his expression relaxed into a sardonic smile.

"I bet they feel *small!*" he said to the umbrella stand.

He went to the library, where his seventeen-year-old brother Robert was showing off his new rifle to a friend.

"You see—" he was saying, then, catching sight of William's face round the door, "Oh, get out!"

William got out.

He returned to his mother in the kitchen with a still more jaundiced view of life. It was still raining. His mother was looking at the tradesmen's books.

"Can I go out?" he said gloomily.

"No, of course not. It's pouring."

"I don't mind rain."

"Don't be silly."

William considered that few boys in the whole world were handicapped by more unsympathetic parents than he.

"Why," he said pathetically, "have they got friends in an' me not?"

"I suppose you didn't think of asking anyone," she said calmly.

"Well, can I have someone now?"

"No, it's too late," said Mrs Brown, raising her head from the butcher's book and murmuring "ten and elevenpence" to herself.

"Well, when can I?"

She raised a harassed face.

"William, do be quiet! Any time, if you ask. Eighteen and twopence."

"Can I have lots?"

"Oh, go and ask your father."

William went out.

He returned to the dining room, where his father was still reading a paper. The sigh with which his father greeted his entrance was not one of relief.

"If you've come to ask questions—" he began threateningly.

"I haven't," said William quickly. "Father, when you're all away on Saturday, can I have a party?"

"No, of course not," said his father irritably. "Can't you *do* something?"

William, goaded to desperation, burst into a flood of eloquence.

"The sort of things I want to do they don't want me to do an' the sort of things I don't want to do they want me to do. Mother said to knit. *Knit*!"

His scorn and fury were indescribable. His father looked out of the window.

"Thank Heaven, it's stopped raining! Go out!"

William went out.

There were some quite interesting things to do outside. In the road there were puddles, and the sensation of walking through a puddle, as every boy knows, is a very pleasant one. The hedges, when shaken, sent quite a shower bath upon the shaker, which also is a pleasant sensation. The ditch was full and there was the thrill of seeing how often one could jump across it without going in. One went in more often than not. It is also fascinating to walk in mud, scraping it along with one's boots. William's spirits rose, but he could not shake off the idea of the party. Quite suddenly he wanted to have a party and he wanted to have it on Saturday. His family would be away on Saturday. They were going to spend the day with an aunt. Aunts rarely included William in their invitation.

He came home wet and dirty and cheerful. He approached his father warily.

"Did you say I could have a party, Father?" he said casually.

"*No*, I did *not*," said Mr Brown firmly.

William let the matter rest for the present.

He spent most of the English Grammar class in school next morning considering it. There was a great deal to be said for a party in the absence of one's parents and grown-up brother and sister. He'd like to ask George and Ginger and Henry and Douglas and . . .

and . . . and . . . heaps of them. He'd like to ask them all. "They" were the whole class – thirty in number.

"What have I just been saying, William?"

William sighed. That was the foolish sort of question that schoolmistresses were always asking. They ought to know themselves what they'd just been saying better than anyone. *He* never knew. Why were they always asking him? He looked blank. Then:

"Was it anythin' about participles?" He remembered something vaguely about participles, but it mightn't have been today.

Miss Jones groaned.

"That was ever so long ago, William," she said. "You've not been attending."

William cleared his throat with a certain dignity and made no answer.

"Tell him, Henry."

Henry ceased his enthralling occupation of trying to push a fly into his inkwell with his nib and answered mechanically:

"Two negatives make an affirmative."

"Yes. Say that, William."

William repeated it without betraying any great interest in the fact.

"Yes. What's a negative, William?"

William sighed.

"Somethin' about photographs?" he said obligingly.

"*No*," snapped Miss Jones. She found William and the heat (William particularly) rather trying. "It's 'no' and 'not'. And an affirmative is 'yes'."

"Oh," said William politely.

"So two 'nos' and 'nots' mean 'yes', if they're in the same sentence. If you said 'There's not no money in the box' you mean there is."

William considered.

He said "Oh" again.

Then he seemed suddenly to become intelligent.

"Then," he said, "if you say 'no' and 'not' in the same sentence does it mean 'yes'?"

"Certainly."

William smiled.

William's smile was a rare thing.

"Thank you," he said.

Miss Jones was quite touched. "It's all right, William," she said. "I'm glad you're beginning to take an interest in your work."

William was murmuring to himself.

"'No, of course *not*' and 'No, I did not' and a 'no' an' a 'not' mean a 'yes', so he meant 'Yes, of course' and 'Yes, I did.'"

He waited till the Friday before he gave his invitations with a casual air.

"My folks is goin' away tomorrow an' they said I could have a few fren's in to tea. Can you come? Tell your mother they said jus' to come an' not bother to write."

He was a born strategist. Not one of his friends' parents guessed the true state of affairs. When William's conscience (that curious organ) rose to reproach him, he said to it firmly:

"He *said* I could. He said '*Yes*, of course.' He said 'Yes, I did.'"

He asked them *all*. He thought that while you are having a party you might as well have a big one. He hinted darkly at unrestrained joy and mirth. They all accepted the invitation.

William's mother took an anxious farewell of him on Saturday morning.

"You don't mind being left, darling, do you?"

"No, Mother," said William with perfect truth.

"You won't do anything we've told you not to, will you?"

"No, Mother. Only things you've said 'yes' to."

Cook and Jane had long looked forward to this day. There would be very little to do in the house and as far as William was concerned they hoped for the best.

William was out all the morning. At lunch he was ominously quiet and polite. Jane decided to go with her young man to the pictures.

Cook said she didn't mind being left, as "that Master William" had gone out and there seemed to be no prospect of his return before teatime.

So Jane went to the pictures.

About three o'clock the postman came and cook went to the door for the letters. Then she stood gazing down the road as though transfixed.

William had collected his guests en route. He was bringing them joyfully home with him. Clean and starched and prim had they issued from their homes, but they had grown hilarious under William's benign influence. They had acquired sticks and stones and old tins from the ditches as they came along. They perceived from William's general attitude towards it that it was no ordinary party. They were a happy crowd. William headed them with a trumpet.

They trooped in at the garden gate. Cook, pale and speechless, watched them. Then her speechlessness departed.

"You're not coming in here!" she said fiercely. "What've you brought all those boys cluttering up the garden?"

"They've come to tea," said William calmly.

She grew paler still.

"That they've *not!*" she said fiercely. "What your father'd say—"

"He *said* they could come," said William. "I asked him an' he said 'Yes, of course', an' I asked if he'd said so an' he said 'Yes, I did.' That's what he said 'cause of English Grammar an' wot Miss Jones said."

Cook's answer was to slam the door in his face and lock it. The thirty guests were slightly disconcerted, but not for long.

"Come on!" shouted William excitedly.

"She's the enemy. Let's storm her ole castle."

The guests' spirits rose. This promised to be infinitely superior to the usual party.

They swarmed round to the back of the house. The enemy had bolted the back door and was fastening all the windows. Purple with fury she shook her fist at William through the drawing-room window. William brandished his piece of stick and blew his trumpet in defiant reply. The army had armed itself with every kind of weapon, including the raspberry canes whose careful placing was the result of a whole day's work of William's father. William decided to climb up to the balcony outside Ethel's open bedroom window with the help of his noble band. The air was full of their defiant war-whoops. They filled the front garden, trampling on all the rose beds, cheering William as he swarmed up to the balcony, his trumpet between his lips. The enemy appeared at the window and shut it with a bang, and William, startled, dropped down among his followers. They raised a hoarse roar of anger.

"Mean ole cat!" shouted the enraged general.

The blood of the army was up. No army of thirty strong worthy of its name could ever consent to be worsted by an enemy of one. All the doors and windows were bolted. There was only one thing to be done. And this the general did, encouraged by loyal cheers from his army. "Go it, ole William! Yah! He – oo – o!"

The stone with which William broke the drawing-room window fell upon a small occasional table, scattering Mrs Brown's cherished silver far and wide.

William, with the born general's contempt for the minor devastations of war, enlarged the hole and helped his gallant band through with only a limited number of cuts and scratches. They were drunk with the thrill of battle. They left the garden with its wreck of rose trees and its trampled lawn and crowded through the broken window with imminent danger to life and limb. The enemy was shutting the small window of the coal cellar, and there William imprisoned her, turning the key with a loud yell of triumph.

The party then proceeded.

It fulfilled the expectations of the guests that it was to be a party unlike any other party. At other parties they played Hide and Seek – with smiling but firm mothers and aunts and sisters stationed at intervals with damping effects upon one's spirits, with 'not in the bedrooms, dear', and 'mind the umbrella stand', and 'certainly not in the drawing room', and 'don't shout so loud, darling'. But this was Hide and Seek from the realms of perfection. Up the stairs and down the stairs, in all the bedrooms, sliding down the balusters, in and out of the drawing room, leaving trails of muddy boots and shattered ornaments as they went!

Ginger found a splendid hiding place in Robert's bed, where his boots left a perfect impression of their muddy soles in several places. Henry found another in Ethel's wardrobe, crouching upon her satin evening shoes among her evening dresses. George banged the drawing-room door with such violence that the handle came off in his hand. Douglas became entangled in the dining-room curtain, which yielded to his struggles and descended upon him and an old china bowl upon the sideboard. It was such a party as none of them had dreamed of; it was bliss undiluted. The house was full of shouting and yelling, of running to and fro of small boys mingled with subterranean murmurs of cook's rage. Cook was uttering horrible imprecations and hurling lumps of coal at the door. She was Irish and longed to return to the fray.

It was William who discovered first that it was teatime and there was no tea. At first he felt slightly aggrieved. Then he thought of the larder and his spirits rose.

"Come on!" he called. "All jus' get what you can."

They trooped in, panting, shouting, laughing, and all just got what they could.

Ginger seized the remnants of a cold ham and picked the bone, George with great gusto drank a whole jar of cream, William and

Douglas between them ate a gooseberry pie, Henry ate a whole currant cake. Each foraged for himself. They ate two bowls of cold vegetables, a joint of cold beef, two pots of honey, three dozen oranges, three loaves and two pots of dripping. They experimented upon lard, onions, and raw sausages. They left the larder a place of gaping emptiness. Meanwhile cook's voice, growing hoarser and hoarser as the result of the inhalation of coal dust and exhalation of imprecations, still arose from the depths and still the door of the coal cellar shook and rattled.

Then one of the guests who had been in the drawing-room window came back.

"She's coming home!" he shouted excitedly.

They flocked to the window.

Jane was bidding a fond farewell to her young man at the side gate.

"Don't let her come in!" yelled William. "Come on!"

With a smile of blissful reminiscence upon her face Jane turned in at the gate. She was totally unprepared for being met by a shower of missiles from upper windows.

A lump of lard hit her on the ear and knocked her hat onto one side. She retreated hastily to the side gate.

"Go on! Send her into the road."

A shower of onions, the ham bone, and a few potatoes pursued her into the road. Shouts of triumph rent the air. Then the shouts of triumph died away abruptly. William's smile also faded away, and his hand, in the act of flinging an onion, dropped. A cab was turning in at the front gate. In the sudden silence that fell upon the party, cook's hoarse cries for vengeance rose with redoubled force from the coal cellar. William grew pale.

The cab contained his family.

Two hours later a small feminine friend of William's who had called with a note for his mother, looked up to William's window and caught sight of William's untidy head.

"Come and play with me, William," she called eagerly.

"I can't. I'm goin' to bed," said William sternly.

"Why? Are you ill, William?"

"No."

"Well, why are you going to bed, William?"

William leant out of the window.

"I'm goin' to bed," he said, "'cause my father don't understand 'bout English Grammar, that's why!"

The Night the Bed Fell

James Thurber

James Thurber grew up in Ohio, America, and in his books he describes many funny episodes from his childhood. This is one of them.

It happened, then, that my father had decided to sleep in the attic one night, to be away where he could think. My mother opposed the notion strongly because, she said, the old wooden bed up there was unsafe: it was wobbly and the heavy headboard would crash down on Father's head in case the bed fell, and kill him. There was no dissuading him, however, and at a quarter past ten he closed the attic door behind him and went up the narrow twisting stairs. We later heard ominous creakings as he crawled into bed. Grandfather, who usually slept in the attic bed when he was with us, had disappeared some days before. (On these occasions he was usually gone six or eight days and returned growling and out of temper, with the news that the federal Union was run by a passel of blockheads and that the Army of the Potomac didn't have any more chance than a fiddler's bitch.)

We had visiting us at this time a nervous first cousin of mine named Briggs Beall, who believed that he was likely to cease breathing when he was asleep. It was his feeling that if he were not awakened every hour during the night, he might die of suffocation. He had been accustomed to setting an alarm clock to ring at intervals until morning, but I persuaded him to abandon this. He slept in my room and I told him that I was such a light sleeper that if anybody quit breathing in the same room with me, I would wake instantly. He tested me the first night – which I had suspected he would – by holding his breath after my regular breathing had convinced him I was asleep. I was not asleep, however, and called to him. This seemed to allay his fears a little, but he took the precaution of putting a glass of spirits of camphor on a little table at the head of his bed. In case I didn't arouse him until he was almost gone, he said, he would sniff the camphor, a powerful reviver . . .

By midnight we were all in bed. The layout of the rooms and the disposition of their occupants is important to an understanding of what later occurred. In the front room upstairs (just under Father's attic bedroom) were my mother and my brother Herman, who sometimes sang in his sleep, usually "Marching Through Georgia" or "Onward, Christian Soldiers". Briggs Beall and myself were in a room adjoining this one. My brother Roy was in a room across the hall from ours. Our bull terrier, Rex, slept in the hall.

My bed was an army cot, one of those affairs which are made wide enough to sleep on comfortably only by putting up, flat with the middle section, the two sides which ordinarily hang down like the sideboards of a drop-leaf table. When these sides are up, it is perilous to roll too far toward the edge, for then the cot is likely to tip completely over, bringing the whole bed down on top of one, with a tremendous banging crash. This, in fact, is precisely what happened, about two o'clock in the morning. (It was my mother who, in recalling the scene later, first referred to it as "the night the bed fell on your father".)

Always a deep sleeper, slow to arouse (I had lied to Briggs), I was at first unconscious to what had happened when the iron cot rolled me on to the floor and toppled over on me. It left me still warmly bundled up and unhurt, for the bed rested above me like a canopy. Hence I did not wake up, only reached the edge of consciousness and went back. The racket, however, instantly awakened my mother, in the next room, who came to the immediate conclusion that her worst dread was realized: the big wooden bed upstairs had fallen on father. She therefore screamed, "Let's go to your poor father!" It was this shout, rather than the noise of my cot falling, that awakened Herman, in the same room with her. He thought that Mother had become, for no apparent reason, hysterical. "You're all right, Mamma!" he shouted, trying to calm her. They exchanged shout for shout for perhaps ten seconds: "Let's go to your poor father!" and "You're all right!" That woke up Briggs. By this time I was conscious of what was going on, in a vague way, but did not yet realize that I was under my bed instead of on it.

Briggs, awakening in the midst of loud shouts of fear and apprehension, came to the quick conclusion that he was suffocating and that we were all trying to "bring him out". With a low moan, he grasped the glass of camphor at the head of his bed and instead of sniffing it poured it over himself. The room reeked of camphor. "Ugf, ahfg," choked Briggs, like a drowning man, for he had almost succeeded in stopping his breath under the deluge of pungent spirits. He leaped out of bed and groped toward the open window, but he came up against one that was closed. With his hand, he beat out the glass, and I could hear it crash and tinkle on the alleyway below. It was at this juncture that I, in trying to get up, had the uncanny sensation of feeling my bed above me! Foggy with sleep, I now suspected, in my turn, that the whole uproar was being made in a frantic endeavour to extricate me from what must be an unheard-of and perilous situation.

"Get me out of this!" I bawled. "Get me out!" I think I had the nightmarish belief that I was entombed in a mine. "Gugh," gasped Briggs, floundering in his camphor.

By this time my mother, still shouting, pursued by Herman, still shouting, was trying to open the door to the attic, in order to go up and get my father's body out of the wreckage. The door was stuck, however, and wouldn't yield. Her frantic pulls on it only added to the general banging and confusion. Roy and the dog were now up, the one shouting questions, the other barking.

Father, farthest away and soundest sleeper of all, had by this time been awakened by the battering on the attic door. He decided that the house was on fire. "I'm coming, I'm coming!" he wailed in a slow, sleepy voice – it took him many minutes to regain full consciousness. My mother, still believing he was caught under the bed, detected in his "I'm coming!" the mournful resigned note of one who is preparing to meet his maker. "He's dying!" she shouted.

"I'm all right!" Briggs yelled to reassure her. "I'm all right!" He still believed that it was his own closeness to death that was worrying Mother. I found at last the light switch in my room, unlocked the door, and Briggs and I joined the others at the attic door. The dog, who never did like Briggs, jumped for him – assuming that he was the culprit in whatever was going on – and Roy had to throw Rex and hold him. We could hear Father crawling out of bed upstairs. Roy pulled the attic door open with a mighty jerk, and Father came down the stairs, sleepy and irritable but safe and sound. My mother began to weep when she saw him. Rex began to howl. "What in the name of God is going on here?" asked Father.

The situation was finally put together like a gigantic jigsaw puzzle. Father caught a cold from prowling around in his bare feet but there were no other bad results. "I'm glad," said Mother, who always looked on the bright side of things, "that your grandfather wasn't here."

The Good Ogre

Ruth Manning-Sanders

There was once a widow who had an only son, a lad called Durak. Folk said that Durak was a simpleton; but simpleton or no, his mother couldn't afford to keep him. So, like other lads, he had to go out into the world to seek for work.

So he walked along, and he walked along, and he came to a mountain. At the foot of the mountain was a great cave, and at the entrance to the cave sat an ogre. And that ogre was huge enough and ugly enough to make a body faint with terror at the sight of him: his great eyes rolled in his head like fiery wheels, his great body was covered with bristles, and his great flat scaly feet had claws on them instead of toes.

Now Durak's mother had told Durak that when he went out into the world he must mind and be polite to everybody he met. And this was the first body that Durak *had* met; so he off with his hat and made his best bow. "Good day, sir," says he, "I hope I find you in good health this morning? Can you kindly tell me how far it is to the place where I wish to go?"

The ogre opened his great mouth and let out a blast of laughter that blew Durak heels over head. "Mannikin," said the ogre, "what are you called, and where do you wish to go?"

Durak picked himself up, dusted his hat, put it back on his head, took it off again, made another bow, and said, "Mother calls me Durak, sir, for I am not otherwise; and Durak, so I've heard tell, is the name of a fool. And the place I wish to go to is the place where I can find work."

"Will you work for me?" says the ogre.

"Gladly, sir," says Durak.

"And what about wages?" says the ogre.

"Would a penny a year be too much?" says Durak.

At this the ogre roared with laughter again, and Durak fell down again, and picked himself up again, and dusted his hat again, and bowed again. And the ogre said, "A penny a year will suit *me* all right. I have a herd of cows for you to look after, and mornings and evenings you must make me a bowl of porridge. That's all I live on, milk and porridge. I have a delicate digestion," said he with a sigh.

So Durak lived with the ogre and worked for him. It was an easy and pleasant life. He liked sauntering out with the cows to their pasture in the dewy morning, and sauntering back to the cave with them in the evenings. And though at first he burned the ogre's porridge every time he made it, the ogre was patient with him, and he learned better by and by.

And at the end of the first year the ogre gave Durak his penny.

"Will you work for me another year, Durak?"

"Yes," says Durak.

That morning, when Durak drove the cows to pasture he stopped at the ogre's well. What did he do then? He took his penny out of his pocket and threw it into the well. "If that penny doesn't sink," says he, "I shall know that I have served my master truly."

But the penny sank.

"There!" says Durak. "That's because I burned the porridge." And he shook his head and walked on after the cows.

Well, Durak lived for a second year with the ogre, and the days went peacefully by. At the end of the second year he got his second penny. What did he do with it? He threw it into the well after the first one. The penny sank. "There!" says he. "That's because I let my master's fire out once or twice."

So he worked for the ogre yet another year, and at the end of this third year, the ogre took a gold coin out of his left ear and gave it to Durak. "I'm raising your wages, my boy," says he.

But no, Durak wouldn't take the gold coin; he wanted his penny, and he got it. He went to the well and threw this third penny into the water. What happened? The penny floated, and the other two pennies rose to the surface of the water, and floated with the third one.

"Oh ho!" says Durak. "Now I have truly served my master!"

And he scooped all three pennies out of the well and put them in his pocket.

"Durak," says the ogre next morning, "it's time you left me and went to seek your fortune."

"Is it, master?"

"Yes, Durak."

"Well, as you say, master."

"Here's a bag of food for you," says the ogre.

"Thank you, master," says Durak, and slings the bag over his shoulder. Then he said goodbye to the ogre, and wandered off into the world.

He walked along, and he walked along, and by and by he felt hungry. So he sat down and ate up all the food he was carrying in his bag.

Then he got up and walked on again. And he hadn't gone very far when he met an old woman who said she was starving.

"Well then," says Durak, "buy yourself some bread." And he gave her his first penny.

So he walked along, and he walked along, and by and by he met an old beggar man, and he was starving too. So Durak gave the beggar man his second penny, and said, "Buy yourself some bread."

All day he wandered on. He didn't know

where he was going; but, bless me, that didn't trouble him! In the evening he came to the seashore, and on the shore was a little ruined hut. *I will live in this hut*, thinks he. And he went in, curled up on the floor, and fell asleep.

Now there was a seaport nearby, and there were boats coming and going. Durak found work among the boats, loading and unloading, and earned a penny or two to buy bread. And a man gave him a fishing line and some hooks, and showed him how to bait the hooks and set the line along the sand at low water. And of the fish he caught, Durak ate some, and gave the rest away to anyone who asked for them. So he lived, and never gave a thought to what the ogre had said about seeking his fortune. But though he didn't seek it, yet his fortune came to him, as you shall hear.

One day there was a great stir in the seaport. Bakers, butchers, grocery men and fruiterers were scurrying to and fro about the quay, loading provisions into a big ship. The ship belonged to a merchant, who stood on the quay, checking up the goods that were brought to the ship.

Durak went as close as he could get to the ship, and gazed at it in admiration. "That's a fine vessel, your honour," says he to the merchant. "Would your honour be sailing far in her?"

"To the ends of the earth to seek my fortune," says the merchant. He looked at Durak and laughed. "Would you like to invest in my venture?"

"Why not?" says Durak. And he gave the merchant his third penny, which all this time he had kept wrapped up in a handkerchief.

The merchant set sail. He arrived in a foreign port; he sold his goods, made a handsome profit and was about to return home again, when he remembered Durak's penny. *Must buy the poor fool something*, he thought. And seeing a lad who was teasing a big tabby cat, he gave the lad Durak's penny and took the cat.

Then he set sail for home. But a great storm

arose, the merchant's ship was blown this way and that way. He was in danger of foundering when he saw an island ahead, and a port with a fine harbour – though what island and what harbour it was, he hadn't a notion. However he managed to steer his ship into the harbour, and there he waited until the storm had blown over.

Now the island belonged to a duke, who lived in a palace overlooking the harbour. And the duke, who loved company and got but little of it, invited the merchant to take supper and spend the night with him. It was a very grand supper, but the merchant had never felt less inclined to eat; for there were big rats running all over the table, and servants stood behind each chair, beating off the rats with sticks.

After supper the duke showed the merchant to his room for the night.

There was no bed in the room, only a great chest with air holes pierced in the lid. "Yes", sighed the duke, "we all have to sleep in chests, because of the rats."

"But haven't you any cats?" said the merchant.

"Cats?" said the duke. "What are those?"

"I'll show you," says the merchant. And he went to his ship and fetched the big tabby cat which he had bought with Durak's penny.

"You can take the chest away," says he to the duke. "I'll sleep on the floor with the cat."

"But the rats will kill and eat you!" cried the duke.

"Not they!" said the merchant.

Well, there it was. Since the merchant wouldn't sleep in the chest, the duke went away and left him – and lay awake all night, thinking to find nothing of his guest but some gnawed bones in the morning. But in the morning – what did he see? The floor of his guest's room strewn with dead rats, the merchant curled up in his cloak, sound asleep, and the sleeping cat curled up beside him.

"Three times its weight in gold!" cried the duke. "I'll give you three times its weight in gold for that animal!"

So the merchant got the gold, and the duke got the cat; and the storm having blown itself out, the merchant set sail for home. And when he reached his home port, there was Durak standing on the quay.

"Welcome home, your honour!" says Durak, taking off his hat and bowing, "I hope your honour made your honour's fortune?"

"Well, not exactly," says the merchant. "But I traded your penny."

"Ha!" says Durak. "That's good news!"

Now the merchant didn't want to give Durak the big bag of gold he'd got for the cat. He thought he had better use for the gold than Durak had. So he fetched a large flat stone that was part of the ship's ballast. "Here's what I've got for you," said he. And he gave Durak the stone.

Durak was delighted. He dragged the stone back to his little hut, made four legs out of driftwood, and set the stone up as a table. "Now I shall eat my dinner in fine style!" thinks he. And he kindled a fire in the hearth, and set about cooking some fish he had caught. But when the fish was cooked and he brought it to the table – what did he see? His stone had turned into solid gold!

Durak didn't stop to eat his fish. He lifted the table off its legs, and hurried with it back to the merchant. "Sir," said he, "you made a mistake, you have given me too much – take it back!"

Then the merchant was frightened. He remembered he had heard tell that fools were precious to God. "My son," said he, "I have sinned, and heaven has justly rebuked me. With your penny I bought a cat. I sold the cat for a bagful of gold – here, take the gold, take it!" And he handed the bag of gold to Durak, and made him keep the table also.

Durak went back to his hut. What was he to do with the bag of gold? He hadn't a notion. It worried him. It kept him awake at night. For the first time in his life he felt unhappy. And at last he carried the bag of gold down the sand and flung it into the sea.

But, bless me, if the sea didn't wash it in again!

"You'll not get over me that way!" says Durak. And he took the bag into the town, meaning to drop it off the end of the quay into deep water.

At the quayside there was a new ship unloading her cargo. The cargo smelled very sweet. Durak asked the captain what it was.

"Incense," said the captain.

"What's that for?" says Durak.

"Well, you burn it," says the captain. "It makes a sweet smell."

"It smells sweet already," says Durak.

"Ah, but sweeter when burned," says the captain.

"I'd like to smell it burning, then," said Durak. And he bought the whole cargo of incense with his bag of gold, and carried it off, sackful by sackful, on to the sand in the front of his hut.

"There's a fine pile!" says he.

And he set fire to it.

The scent of the burning incense spread far

and wide. The fragrant smoke was drifted by the wind to the ogre's cave. *Sniff, sniff, sniff*!

What's that lad Durak up to now? thought the ogre. And he put on his seven-leagued boots and was outside Durak's hut in a twinkling.

"Durak, my son," says he, "what are you doing?"

So Durak tells him the whole story, and the ogre laughs and says, "What *you* want, my lad, is a clever wife."

"I should like that," says Durak. "But where to find her?"

"See that little rock out there in the water?" says the ogre.

"Yes, I see it."

"Well, you wade out and stand on it," says the ogre. "Watch the fishes swim past. When you see one with a gold ring round its neck, catch it up in your hands and bring it ashore."

"Why?" says Durak.

"Because I tell you to," says the ogre.

So Durak waded out to the rock, and looked down into the water. Fishes swam by, fishes of all colours – red, blue, silver, brown, and grey, speckled, and striped. And at last came one with a gold ring round its neck; and Durak caught it up between his hands and brought it ashore.

"Now I have a pretty fish," said he. "But no wife."

Oh ho, hadn't he? The fish gave a jump out of his two hands. And there at his side stood a beautiful maiden, with a gold ring on her finger.

"I am to be your wife, Durak," says the maiden.

Was Durak delighted? I tell you he was! The maiden took him by the hand and led him up the beach. "Don't look round at the sea till I tell you," said she.

"Why not?" says Durak.

"Because I say you mustn't," said the maiden.

"Well, I won't then," said Durak.

So, when they came near the top of the beach, the maiden said, "*Now* look round, Durak!"

Durak looked round. What did he see? He saw a team of horses, and then a flock of sheep, and then a herd of cows, led by a great bull, all wading out of the water and moving up the beach, orderly as you please.

"Oh ho!" says Durak. "Whose are those?"

"They're ours," says the maiden. "Yours and mine, Durak."

"Oh!" says Durak. "Oh!"

"Well then, just you keep your eye on them," says the maiden. "And don't you look landward till I say so."

Durak stood still, and kept his eye on the

flocks and herds. He thought he must be dreaming.

"Now look to land, Durak!" cried the maiden.

Durak turned round and looked to the land. What did he see? Where his ruined hut had stood amid a tangle of reeds – there, in a pretty garden, stood a cosy little farmhouse with barns and stables. Behind the farmhouse were fields and meadows, and flowing through the meadows was a stream, bordered by willows.

"Oh ho!" says Durak. "Whose house is that?"

"It's ours," said the maiden. "And tomorrow is our wedding day."

So next day Durak and the maiden were married. The ogre put on his seven-leagued boots and fetched Durak's mother to the wedding. The maiden baked a cake, but the ogre couldn't eat any of it, because of his delicate digestion. So the maiden made him some porridge. She poured cream on the porridge, and the ogre gobbled it up. He said it was the best porridge ever he'd tasted.

Harold and Bella, Jammy and Me

Robert Leeson

Harold was a show-off. Whatever you knew, he knew better. Whatever you had, he had better. And he could always win the argument by thumping you, because he was bigger. That was the main reason why we put up with him. Because the gang in the street round the corner from us would have slaughtered us if it hadn't been for Harold. With him around we could slog 'em any time. So, even when he gave you the pip, which was about ten times a day, you put up with him.

As I said, whatever was going new, his family had to have it first – sliced bread, gate-legged tables, copper fire-irons, zip fasteners. They had rubber hot-water bottles when the rest of us still had a hot brick in an old sock, a gas cooker when our mams still cooked on the open range, an electric iron when Mam still heated her iron on the fire and spat on it to test the heat. They were first to have a five-shilling flip in a monoplane at Blackpool and they were first to have the telephone put in round our way. That was a dead loss because there was almost no one to ring up. It was sickening all round, the way they carried on. But worst of all was when they got the wireless.

Mr Marconi's invention was slow to arrive in Tarcroft. That is if you didn't count the crystal sets owned by the doctor and the man who hired out the charabanc. Most people couldn't afford the wireless at first. But, of course, when Mr Marconi did arrive round our way, he came to Harold's house first.

We were sitting, the four of us, one day in the branches of the old oak tree that stands in the meadows at the top of the lane, when

Harold spoke up:

"We're getting a wireless."

There was silence for a second or two. What could you say? Then, just as Harold was going to speak again, Jammy said:

"So are we."

"Get off. You're a little ligger, Jammy."

"Am not."

"Are."

"Want to bet?" asked Jammy, and he stretched himself out along his branch with hands behind his head, lying balanced. I don't know how he dared do it, twenty feet up.

"Want to bet?" he repeated.

Harold kept his mouth shut a minute, then burst out:

"All right, what make is it?"

"Cossor."

"They're no good. Ours is a Philips."

"Get off. Cossor are better than Philips any day."

"Not."

"Are."

Bella made a face at me. Harold went on:

"Our wireless pole's twenty-five foot high."

"Ours is thirty foot," said Jammy.

"It never."

"'Tis' n' all."

"How d'you know?"

"Because our dad climbed it when he fixed the aerial."

Harold laughed like a drain.

"I always knew you were a monkey – that proves it."

Jammy retorted: "I bet your dad couldn't climb the clothes post."

"My dad wouldn't mess about climbing a wireless pole like a chimpanzee. We had a man in to fix ours. I bet your dad didn't buy a wireless. Bet he put it together with bits and pieces."

That was getting near the mark. Jammy's dad was always fixing things.

"He never," said Jammy, but he looked a bit funny.

"OK," went on Harold. "Bet you can't get Radio Luxembourg."

"Can a duck swim? Course we can."

"All right. What do you listen in to?"

"Ovaltineys."

"They're no good. Joe the Sanpic Man's miles better."

"Him? He's barmy, like you."

"You're crackers."

"You two give me a headache," snapped Bella. But Harold wouldn't give up.

"How big's your wireless cabinet?" he asked craftily.

"How big's yours?" asked Jammy.

"Ya ha," sneered Harold. "You daren't say because ours is bigger and you know it."

"Want to bet?" said Jammy. But I had a feeling he was getting desperate.

"OK. How much?" Harold was sure of himself and I began to feel sorry for Jammy.

"Ten to one." Jammy was getting wild now.

"What in, conkers?"

"No, tanners."

"You never, that's a dollar if you lose."

Bella climbed down to a lower branch, hung on for a moment with her hands, then dropped to the ground.

"I'm off."

I jumped down after her and Jammy followed. He was mad. Harold was laughing at him and I knew Jammy was making it up. Next day, though, we all went down to the Clough and played sliding in the old sandpit. It was smashing. I thought the stupid bet had been forgotten. I hated quarrels and so did Bella. But Harold hadn't forgotten at all.

Next week, Bella came round after school. That Wednesday there was to be a wedding in the Royal Family. School was closed for a half day. Would we like to come round and listen to it on their wireless? I thought to myself, Harold's mam's as bad as he is.

When we got round there on the day, there was quite a crowd in their front room. Jammy's mother was there and some other women from our street and even one from round the corner.

She wore a funny big hat and had a put-on accent.

"Oh, I see you've had your sofa covered in rexine."

"Oh, yes," said Harold's mam, "it's the latest thing for *settees*." She said the word "settee" a bit louder, but the other woman didn't seem to notice.

"I'm not sure I fancy rexine, myself. It makes your drawers stick to your bottom."

"Would you care for a cup of tea?" Harold's mam said quickly to our mam, who was staring out of the window to hide a smile.

While all this was going on, Harold was nudging Jammy and pointing to the corner. There on a special table stood the wireless, a big brown walnut cabinet with ornamental carving over the loudspeaker part and a line of polished buttons along the bottom. I thought Jammy looked sick. That wireless was enormous. It must have been two feet high and a foot across. Harold's mother switched on. There was a lot of crackling and spitting.

"Just atmospherics," she said.

Jammy looked more cheerful. Perhaps it wouldn't work. But it did. Harold's mother gave the cabinet a very unladylike thump on

the top and the crackling stopped. We could hear an organ playing and an old bloke droning on about something, then some singing, then a lot more crackling. Another hefty bang on the top and we heard a bloke with a posh voice telling us what we'd been listening to, in case we hadn't got it. I didn't think much to it all, but mam and the other women said it was lovely. Then Jammy's mother piped up.

"On Saturday afternoon, I'd like you all round to our house for a cup of tea. There's a nice music programme we can listen in to."

Harold's mother looked a bit peeved but smiled and said: "Delighted." But Jammy looked green.

Harold sniggered and whispered, "That'll cost you a dollar."

When we got outside I said; "Hey, Harold, this bet's daft. Jammy hasn't got a dollar. It'll take him months to save that up."

Bella nodded. But Harold smirked.

"Serve him right. He should keep his big mouth shut." He turned round and swung on the gate. "See you on Saturday, Jammy – have the money ready. I'll take two half dollars, or five bobs, ten tanners or twenty three-penny joeys. But not sixty pennies, 'cause it weighs your pockets down."

Jammy slouched off down the road by himself.

Saturday teatime came round all too soon and there we were in Jammy's kitchen. They didn't have a front room. Jammy's mother had a good fire going, though it was the middle of July, and the kettle was boiling. The table was loaded with bread and butter, meat paste and corned beef sandwiches, and scones. We all sat down. Harold looked all round him, a fat grin on his face.

"Where's the wireless, missis?"

"You speak when you're spoken to," said his mam.

"That's quite all right," said Jammy's mam. "Alan, just take the dust cloth off will you, love."

Jammy nipped sharply up from the table and whipped away a cloth that was hanging in the corner. I heard Harold choke on a mouthful of bread and butter. We all stared as Jammy switched on and the music came through with hardly any crackling.

But the cabinet! It must have been five foot high, not on a table, but standing on the floor. The loudspeaker part was decorated with cream-coloured scroll work. Below were two sets of knobs and switches that seemed to go all the way down to the floor.

"Another butty, Harold?" Jammy said sweetly. Bella and I sniggered. Mam tapped me on the head and said "Sh!"

As soon as tea was over, Harold made an excuse and dashed out first. By the time we got to the door, he was heading off up the road.

"Whatever did our Harold dash off like that for?" asked his mother.

"Gone to dig up his money box, I should think," chuckled Bella.

"I shall never understand what you have to giggle so much for, child. Come along," said Bella's mam, and swept away down the path, followed by Bella.

I turned to Jammy, who was his normal cheerful self.

"You won that one, Jammy," I said. "What are you going to do with that five bob?"

He grinned. "Nowt. He can keep it. It was worth it just to see that look on his face. Besides," he added and whispered in my ear, "it wasn't a real wireless cabinet. It was an old second-hand kitchen cabinet. Dad did it up and fitted our wireless into the top part."

"But what about all those knobs?"

"Oh, he put them on for show. He uses the bottom part to keep his beer in."

I laughed all the way home.

Any time after that, when Jammy wanted to annoy Harold all he had to say was, "Same to you – with knobs on!"

The Paw Thing

Paul Jennings

Major Mac's takeaway chicken joint had a cat that couldn't catch mice. She ran after them. She jumped at them. She tried her best but the poor old thing just couldn't catch a mouse. Not one.

The cat's name was Singenpoo.

"It's the worst mouser in the world," said Mac. "I don't know why I keep it." From the way he spoke it sounded as if Mac didn't like the cat at all. I felt sorry for her but I didn't say anything because it was my first day working at Major Mac's. After-school jobs were hard to find and I didn't want to get the sack.

I had never heard of a cat called Singenpoo

before. I found out later how she got her name. It seems that Mac once had this tiny transistor radio. A real small one. It was about half the size of a matchbox. One day Mac changed the station after he had been cutting up fish. The cat noticed that the radio had a fishy smell and she started licking it. Before Mac could blink, the cat had swallowed the whole thing.

At first Mac was mad at the cat. He shook her this way and that trying to get her to cough up the radio, but nothing happened. It wouldn't come out. Then he heard something strange. Music. Music was coming out of the cat's mouth. Mac grinned. He made the cat sit on the chair with her mouth open so that he could listen to the radio. Every day after that the poor old cat had to sit next to Mac with her mouth open. Mac would listen to the footy on Saturdays. In the mornings he listened to the news at seven o'clock. On Sundays the cat was tuned in to the top forty.

Everyone thought it was really funny. Except the cat. She had to follow Mac around everywhere with her mouth open so that he could have music wherever he went.

Then one day the music stopped.

"Drat," said Mac, giving the cat a shake. "The battery's dead." At that very moment he heard a faint singing noise coming from outside. He dropped the poor cat on the floor and went out the door. The music was coming from the cat's sand tray. There, in the kitty litter, was a little bit of square cat poo. The radio was in the cat poo. The cat poo was singing a song called "Please Release Me, Let Me Go".

Mac was cross. He picked up the singing poo and flushed it down the toilet.

And that's how the cat came to be called Singenpoo.

Every night the cat ate her tea from a chipped bowl. The bowl had SINGENPOO written on the side in big letters. Not that she got much tea. Mac just didn't look after her properly. He was mad at her because she didn't play tunes any more and she couldn't catch mice. Sometimes when Mac wasn't looking I would throw a bit of fried chicken to Singenpoo. She would look up at me, almost as if she was smiling. Then she would gobble up the chicken as quickly as she could.

All Mac gave her to eat was raw chicken claws and beaks. "It doesn't earn its keep," said Mac. "If it caught mice I would give it a drumstick or two. I keep it hungry. That way it might try a bit harder."

On my first day Mac showed me over the front of the shop. Out the front they had a place where the customers queued up.

"You stand here, Scott," said Mac. "You take the customer's order and then you repeat it into this microphone. I will be out the back packing the chicken into boxes. When I finish each one I will push the box through this little window. You give it to the customers and take their money."

He took me out the back and showed me where the chickens were cooked. There were big ovens and vats for frying chickens. There was also a cool-room where the fresh batches of chickens were stored. On one of the walls was a safe with a combination lock on the front.

"Is that for the money?" I asked Mac.

"No," he replied. He opened up the safe and took out a black book. On the cover it said:

MAJOR MAC's
SECRET FRIED CHICKEN RECIPE
of
Fifty Different Burps and Spices

"No one," said Mac in a gruff voice, "is allowed to touch this book. No one." He lowered his voice and looked around. "There are people who would pay big money for what's in this book. Customers come from miles around for my special fried chicken. There is a new chicken place opening up on the other side of town called the Dead Rooster. If they get my secret recipe we will be out of business." He put the book back in the safe.

"When this book is open," he went on, "you

stay out the front. Nobody comes into the kitchen when this book is open, Scott." Then he said something weird. Really weird. He pointed at Singenpoo. "You stay away from the book too, cat. No one reads the secret recipe but me." He looked at Singenpoo as if he really thought the cat could read the book.

Well, things went along OK for about a month. I soon got the hang of working the till and taking orders. Whenever the secret recipe book was open I stayed out of the kitchen. I didn't want Mac thinking I was trying to pinch his secret recipe.

Mac was a little bit odd but he was right about one thing. His fried chicken sure was popular. People bought it by the barrelful. They loved it. I was flat-out trying to serve the hungry crowd that turned up every night.

But poor old Singenpoo got thinner and thinner. I tried to throw her the odd chicken wing when Mac wasn't watching but that wasn't often.

"Beaks and claws," said Mac. "That's all it gets until it starts catching mice. There are more of them every day."

There were, too. When I first started you would see the odd mouse out behind the rubbish bins. After a while, though, they got cheekier and cheekier. They would even run across the floor between the customers' legs. One lady screamed as a mouse ran over her shoes. She fled out of the shop screaming something about getting the health inspector.

"Useless cat," yelled Mac. "From now on you only get beaks. No claws. See if that will help you to run a bit faster."

Singenpoo looked up at me with sad eyes. She was all skin and bone. She seemed to be asking me for help but there was nothing I could do. Mac was the boss. The skinnier Singenpoo got, the slower she ran. There was no way she was ever going to catch a mouse. And there were more and more of them every time I looked.

*

Then the terrible day came. The Dead Rooster opened up for the first time. They had a big ad in the local paper. They were selling their fried chicken at special low prices.

"Trying to pinch our customers," sniffed Mac. He handed me five dollars. "Go over and buy a bit of their chicken. Bring some back and I will see if it's any good."

I rode my bike over to the Dead Rooster and got in the queue. I bought a Chuckit of Chicken and took it back to Mac. He opened the box and sniffed. Then he took out a chicken wing and had a small nibble. He smacked his lips and made sucking noises. He took another bite and chewed slowly with his eyes closed. I noticed that his face was slowly turning red. He opened his eyes and looked around in rage.

"It's delicious," he screamed. "It's the same as mine. It's my secret recipe of fifty burps and spices. They've nicked our recipe. The ratbags. The mongrels. Somebody's given them our recipe." He glared at me with accusing eyes.

"Don't look at me," I said. "I didn't tell them the secret recipe. I don't want you to go broke. I would be out of a job if you did. I've never touched your book."

Mac spoke slowly. "You're right," he said. He walked over to the safe and opened it. Then he took out the black book and flipped over the pages. One had been torn out. "Ah ha," he yelled. "Just as I thought." He pointed a long skinny finger at Singenpoo. "You're the one. You're the one that gave them the recipe."

Singenpoo crouched down in the corner. She was frightened by all the yelling.

Mac had flipped his lid. He thought the cat had torn the page out of the book with her mouth.

"Don't be silly," I said. "Cats can't read. She wouldn't know which page to take."

"Look at this," shouted Mac. He thrust the book under my nose and pointed at a smudge on the corner of the first page. "A paw print. A paw print. The cat has been at my book."

"So?" I said. "Singenpoo probably jumped up on the table and stepped on the book. That doesn't mean that she read it."

By now Mac was so angry that he was spitting as he spoke. "I tell you, Singenpoo has been reading the recipe book. I have suspected it for weeks. One night I saw it looking at it. And not just looking at it: it turned over the page with its paw."

I started to laugh. I just couldn't help it. The whole idea was crazy.

"Singenpoo has to go," said Mac. "I'm not having the mangy thing here for one more minute." He took twenty dollars out of his wallet. "Take it down to the vet's and have it put down."

"Put down? What do you mean, put down? Put down where?"

"Put down. Put to sleep. Killed," grunted Mac.

I couldn't believe it. "She's innocent," I said. "Cats can't read. Someone else stole your secret recipe. It wasn't Singenpoo. Don't have her put down. Please." I picked up the frightened cat and held her in my arms.

Mac pointed to the door. "Even if it didn't read the book," he said, "it can't catch mice. It's no good to us. Go, or you are sacked."

I took the twenty dollars and walked out of the door with Singenpoo still in my arms. She was shivering with fear. Cats can tell when something is wrong. I looked around for somewhere to hide her. There was no way that I was going to have her put to sleep.

Over the back fence of the chicken shop was an empty shed. An old lady called Mrs Griggs owned it. I knew she never went near the shed because it was right down the bottom of her garden. She didn't need the shed. I jumped the fence and put Singenpoo inside.

"For goodness sake, don't start to miaow," I said. "I'll come back every night and bring you chicken legs and milk." I stayed with her for about half an hour. Then I shut the shed door and went back to Mac's.

Mac never said anything when I went back. He didn't even ask me for the change. I think he was feeling guilty about Singenpoo.

Every night after that I crept down to the shed and fed Singenpoo on fried chicken and milk. She got fatter and fatter.

Things were not so good at Major Mac's Fried Chicken Shop, though. More and more mice arrived with every passing day. We had a terrible job keeping them out of sight. Mac didn't want the customers to see the mice. They were in bins and behind the fridge. At night-time they slithered across the floor right in front of our eyes. We chased them around with brooms but they weren't even scared of us.

We had hundreds of mousetraps. Each morning it was my job to empty them and put the dead mice into the rubbish. Mac invented a new type of trap. He got an empty beer bottle and put a piece of cheese in the end. Then he laid the bottle on its side with the neck sticking out over the edge of the table. He smeared butter along the neck of the bottle. On the floor underneath was a bin filled with water. When the mice walked along the neck of the bottle to get the cheese they lost their footing and fell into the bin. In the mornings we would find about two hundred drowned mice in the bin. It was really bad. And it was getting worse.

One Saturday when I was serving customers at the front bench, a bald-headed man came back with his chicken roll. He had eaten about half of it. He was a pretty rude bloke because he yelled at me with his mouth full.

"I didn't order sesame seeds on my roll,"

he said, waving the half-eaten roll in my face.

"We don't have sesame seeds on our rolls," I answered.

He looked at his chicken roll carefully. Then he ran outside and spat out what he had been eating.

"Arghhhh. Arghhhh," he yelled. "Mouse droppings. Filthy mouse droppings on my chicken roll. You'll pay for this. I'll have this place closed down." He ran around in circles holding his hands up to his throat.

All the customers left. Fast.

On a sign outside was written:

DROP IN
FOR A
CHICKEN ROLL

A kid who was with the bald-headed man went up to the sign and wrote on it with a texta. He put in some extra letters. Now it read:

DROPPINGS
FOR A
CHICKEN ROLL

Not long after, the health inspector arrived. He took one look at the mice running all over the floor and shelves of the kitchen and said, "I am closing this place down. You can't serve food from a store that's infested with mice."

He slapped a notice on the window that said:

CLOSED
Due to Mouse Plague

Then he jumped in his car and drove off. Mac hung his head in his hands. "Ruined," he wailed. "Ruined. We have to get rid of these mice or we'll go broke." Then he looked at the cool-room door. "Oh no," he went on. "The warning light is off. The mice must have eaten through the electricity wires. All the chickens in the cool-room will be ruined.

There's eight hundred frozen chickens in that cool-room."

He walked over and pulled open the cool-room door. There were no chickens in there. There were about ten million mice. They poured out in a great wave that was at least as high as Mac's head. We both screamed as the front of the mouse-wave hit us and knocked us over. They flooded out into the kitchen and covered the floor, the benches and even the walls. A great squirming, wriggling, squeaking river.

I could feel mice running up my trousers. They wriggled under my shirt and my singlet. They were even inside my underpants. They were chewing at my clothes. Mouse heads were sticking out of holes that they had eaten in my T-shirt. The leg of one of my jeans had disappeared altogether and the other was following it fast.

I could hear Mac shouting at the top of his voice. He was pulling mice out of his hair as he waded towards the door through the

knee-high sea of rodents. They had nearly eaten his shirt clean off his back.

I struggled after him as quickly as I could and we both fled panting into the back of the yard. We jumped up and down, shaking out the nibbling pests and stamping on them. When we had got the last ones out we lay on the ground looking at the fried-chicken shop in disbelief. Through the windows we could see the whole thing was crawling with mice. It was like looking at a giant jar filled with wriggling beans. I didn't know that there were that many mice in the whole world.

Just then a soft "miaow" came from over the fence.

"What was that?" asked Mac.

"It's Singenpoo," I said.

Mac looked at me. "How could it be?" he said, glaring at me through narrow eyes. "Singenpoo is dead."

"I couldn't do it, Mac," I said. "I just couldn't have her put to sleep. I've been hiding her in that shed." I looked at the millions of mice. "Even Singenpoo could catch a mouse today. I'll go and get her."

I jumped over the fence and fetched Singenpoo from the shed. Then I took her to the back door of the chicken shop and put her down.

"Go get 'em, Singenpoo," I said. I half expected her to run off as fast as she could go. I mean, what could one cat do against millions of mice?

The answer is: plenty.

Singenpoo walked into that chicken shop with her tail held up in the air. She gave a couple of quick, low hisses that seemed to freeze the mice. They dropped off the walls and shelves and moved away from her like a living carpet. She herded them out of the kitchen, running this way and that, darting, skipping, nipping and hissing. They seethed out into the shop and burst onto the road.

Singenpoo stood waiting for them all to get out. It took a long time, but at last they all passed through the door. Every single one. A couple of thousand made a sudden dart and tried to get back in, but Singenpoo was too quick for them. She rounded them up and herded them back with the main mob.

Mac and I just stood there gasping. We couldn't believe it. It was incredible.

The cars in the street stopped. People ran into the shops and shut the doors. They peered out of their windows and watched as Singenpoo moved the plague of squealing mice down the main street. Just as they reached the traffic lights the mob divided in two groups and one lot headed off towards the butcher's shop. I gasped. She had lost control. In a flash Singenpoo skipped lightly over the backs of the teeming horde and darted in and out, driving them back with the rest. She reminded me of a sheepdog herding sheep on a farm.

Without so much as a miaow she headed the mice off towards the beach. Along the street, past the library, and down by Lake Pertobe. The herd squealed and scampered but there was no escape. Singenpoo drove them out onto the breakwater and along to the end of the pier.

They tumbled and jumbled. An endless grey waterfall of mice plunging off the end of the pier and into the sea. In the end, every last one was gone. Drowned. Dead. Done for.

"You beauty," yelled Mac. "You little ripper. You've saved the day. Singenpoo, the fabulous feline." He hoisted her up onto his shoulder. The whole town was there, cheering and clapping. The crowd went crazy with joy. Especially the butcher.

A photographer from the *Standard* took photos. Everyone wanted to stroke and pat Singenpoo.

After a long time we got back to the shop.

"From now on," said Mac, "this cat has the best of everything. And the first thing I am going to do is give her a big feed. Where's her bowl?"

"In the shed," I told him.

We climbed over the fence and went into the shed where Singenpoo had been locked up. Mac got Singenpoo's bowl and looked around the empty shed.

"What's this?" he asked. He picked up a dusty book and peered at it. The book had smudged paw marks on the pages.

"I didn't notice that there," I said. "It must belong to Mrs Griggs. What's it called?"

Mac turned the book over and read out the title in a whispered voice. It was called *How to Train a Sheepdog*.

Oonagh

Robert Leeson

Oonagh lived on Knockmany Hill with her ever-loving husband Fin M'Coul.

No one knew why Fin had built their house up there among the clouds, where the wind blew day and night. He said he enjoyed the view, though Oonagh suspected there was some other reason he wasn't telling her about.

Worse still, there was no water to be had on the hilltop. Fin was always promising to sink a well. But it never got dug.

And where was he now? At the other end of Ireland with a band of other giants building a great rock causeway over the sea to Scotland!

To while away the time in his absence,

Oonagh chatted now and then with her sister Granua, who lived on Cullamore across the valley. It was three or four miles away, but that was no problem if they just raised their voices a little.

One evening Granua said, "Would you believe it, sister? Who d'you think's coming up the road, no more than fifty miles away."

"Tell me, sister, tell me."

"Why, your ever-loving man, Fin M'Coul."

"What can he want now? Surely they've not built all the way over to Scotland already?"

"You'll find out soon enough, sister," said Granua.

Sure enough, before the sun was down, in through the door came Fin, calling out, "God save all here."

"Welcome home, Fin my darling," said Oonagh, giving him a kiss that stirred up waves on the lake down at the foot of Knockmany.

"And how are you, beautiful one?" asked her husband.

"As merry a wife as ever there was,"

answered Oonagh. "And what brings you home so soon?"

Fin looked at her a little oddly but laughed. "Just love and affection for yourself, you know that."

But after two or three happy days had passed, Oonagh, who was nobody's fool, could see something was wrong with her husband. So she set to work to wheedle it out of him. And at last he confessed.

"It's this Cucullin. For months he's been rampaging round Ireland looking to destroy me. They say he's flattened a thunderbolt to a pancake and carries it in his pocket to show what he's going to do to my head – if I let him come near enough."

"So that is why we live up here, Fin?"

"That's it, my love. So I can see him coming."

"But, he's far away, surely to goodness?"

Fin shook his head and put his thumb in his mouth and began to chew it. For his thumb could tell him what or who was to come his way.

"Don't draw blood now, my dear," said his wife.

Fin took out his thumb. "Cucullin's coming. I can see him below Dungannon. He'll be here by two o'clock tomorrow." He groaned. "What shall I do? If I run away, I'm disgraced as a coward. If I stay, I'm dead mutton."

Oonagh looked at him fondly. "Don't be cast down, my love. I'll think of something a bit smarter than your rule of thumb."

She went to the door and called out over the valley, "What can you see, sister?"

Back came the answer, "The biggest giant that ever was, coming up from Dungannon. What can he want, now?"

"He's on his way to leather our Fin!"

"Is he now. Well, Oonagh, I'll invite him in for a meal and detain him a little to give you time to think of something. Knowing you, I'm sure you'll get the better of him."

So saying, Granua put fingers to her lips and gave three whistles, which was a polite way of inviting the unwelcome guest to tarry awhile and take pot luck with her.

Now Oonagh busied herself. She spun threads of nine different colours, dividing them into three plaits. One plait she tied round her arm, one round her heart and one round her ankle. With these charms she was ready for anything and anybody.

Next she set dough and put down a great pot of milk to make curds and whey, while Fin watched her and grumbled, "Are you going to *feed* the brute before he murders me?"

"Oh, Fin, I'm ashamed of you," said his wife. "Leave Cucullin to me. I'll give him a meal like he's never had in his life. Trust Oonagh."

Out she went to her neighbours in the mountains round about – it took her no more than a minute or two – and borrowed twenty-one griddle irons. As she made up the loaves she put an iron inside each, save one. Then she set them all to bake.

"Now, Fin, my lad," said she, "get the baby's clothes on and lie down in the cradle. Pretend to be your own child. Don't say a word. Just listen while I tell you what to do. Trust Oonagh."

Fin was humiliated. But that's a shade better than being flattened. So he did as he was told.

All too soon in walked the giant Cucullin saying, "God save all here. Is this the home of Fin M'Coul?"

"It is," replied Oonagh. "Tell me – from the stern look on your face – is there something wrong concerning my husband?"

"Not at all." Cucullin leered at Oonagh. "It's just that he has the reputation of being strongest in all Ireland and I'd like to put that to the test. But I can't seem to catch up with the man."

"And no wonder," said Oonagh very quickly, "for you're looking in entirely the wrong direction. He heard you were down at the Giant's Causeway and off he went there in a hurry."

"Well," said Cucullin, rising, "when I get my hands on him . . ."

But Oonagh only laughed. "Sit down, now. You never saw Fin, I can tell. And if you'll take my advice, you'll pray that you never do. For he's mad to lay hands on you."

She looked round. "Drat that wind. It's blowing right through the door again and my husband's not here to turn the house round as he always does for me when the wind shifts. Can you be civil enough to do it instead?"

Cucullin's mouth dropped open for a moment. But, not to be outfaced, he got up, cracked his middle finger (where his power lay) three times, then grabbed the house by the corners and swung it around on its foundations.

That shook Oonagh a little, and what it did to Fin, crouched in the cradle, can just be imagined.

"That's decent of you," she said calmly. "Now, before I offer you something to eat, can you do me a second favour? Fin's been so busy lately chasing after you, he's had no time to sink me a well for water. Just four hundred feet would do, no more."

Her guest's jaw dropped at this, but pride would not let him refuse. Out he went, cracked his strength finger nine times and tore a great cleft a quarter of a mile long and four hundred foot deep in the ground, which is still there for anyone to see.

"Now," said Oonagh, satisfied, "pray sit down and eat." She set bacon and cabbage and a great pile of new-baked loaves on the table.

Hungry as a wolf, Cucullin snatched up a loaf and stuffed it into his mouth. But the next moment he was howling with pain and spitting out his best teeth.

"Blood and fury," he bellowed, "what have you put in these loaves?"

Oonagh shrugged. "Why, they're just what my husband – and the baby – always eat. See."

And with that she offered a loaf (the one without a griddle iron in it, of course) to Fin in the cradle. He, falling in with the trick, made it vanish in a trice.

The guest was thunderstruck. "Let's have a look at that infant," he growled.

Oonagh gave Fin the nod and he stepped out of his cradle. He looked a complete fool in the swaddling clothes, but Cucullin did not find him comical at all.

"What size must the father be," he asked, "if this be the child?"

"Pray you'll never find out," said Fin, beginning to enjoy the joke. "In my father's absence, will you go a trial of strength with me? Can you squeeze water out of this little white stone?"

Well, Cucullin squeezed that white stone till he almost burst a blood vessel, but not a drop of moisture came out of it.

Fin now took up a handful of Oonagh's white curds. This he squeezed until the clear whey liquid ran down for all the world like water. Then, with a look of silent contempt for Cucullin, he climbed back into his cradle.

That man's knees now began to knock together. "I'll be off," he said, "and kindly tell your husband I shall make myself scarce and hope not to meet him."

But before he left he could not resist one

last question. "The baby's teeth must be made of iron to eat that bread of yours. Can I have a look at them?"

"You can do more. You can put your middle finger right in and feel them," invited Oonagh.

This he did. And Fin needed no invitation. He closed his teeth and snapped off the visitor's strength finger, clean as a whistle. In

a trice, Cucullin's power was gone, and so was he, running away down the mountain.

So it came about that Cucullin, the terror, ceased to bother Fin. And all thanks to Oonagh.

Miss Pettigrew's Parrot

Richmal Crompton

"**W**on't you reconsider it, dear?" said Mrs Manning.

"No, I won't," said Mr Manning, ramming his hat on his head and snatching up his attaché case. "I've had a basinful from that kid this week, and this is the last straw."

With that he strode angrily down the path, out of the gate and off towards the bus stop.

"That kid" was Roger, and the "basinful" was a broken window on Monday, a cascade of water down the stairs on Tuesday, a campfire on the lawn on Wednesday, a tightrope exhibition, resulting in two broken clothes props, on Thursday and a lion hunt in the lounge on Friday. Today was Saturday, and the "last straw" was a letter, received by the morning's post from a neighbour, Miss Pettigrew, informing him that a football, kicked by Roger in the lane outside her cottage, had gone through her open window and overturned her parrot's cage, freeing the catch, so that the parrot had escaped and had not been seen since. At this, Mr Manning, displaying the natural fury of the male parent goaded beyond endurance, had decreed that Roger was not to go to the circus with the rest of the family in the afternoon.

Gloom pervaded the household. It was Jimmy who showed most open signs of it. Life for Jimmy was always overcast when Roger was in disgrace, and the thought of Roger's being left at home while the rest of them went to the circus was unendurable. Roger himself behaved with a stoical fortitude that increased Jimmy's always fervent hero-worship of him. He went about pale but composed.

"I suppose there'll be other circuses," he said nonchalantly, adding, with a generosity that staggered Jimmy: "The old chap's right from his point of view, of course. One can't really blame him."

But this carefully sustained attitude could not hide from Jimmy the blackness of despair that engulfed Roger's spirit.

And Jimmy determined to do something about it.

He met Bobby Peaslake in the shed at the bottom of the garden. Bobby Peaslake was the little boy who lived opposite. He was the same age as Jimmy but incredibly tall, with arms and legs that never looked adequately clothed, despite his mother's frantic efforts to keep up with them. He always wore on one bony wrist an enormous wristwatch of antique design without works or fingers, which, he fondly imagined, gave him an air of maturity, and he cultivated a man-of-the-world manner that was apt to desert him in times of crisis. The two had already spent several precious hours in a fruitless search for Miss Pettigrew's parrot over the neighbouring countryside.

"Well, if we can't find her ole parrot," said Jimmy, "we've gotter find her something that'll do instead, so that she'll say it's all right an' let Roger go to the circus. What does she want a rotten ole parrot for, anyway?"

"She says it's comp'ny," said Bobby.

"Well, so is anythin' else," said Jimmy. He was silent for a few moments, waging a secret battle with himself, then went on: "If it's comp'ny she wants, Henry's comp'ny. I wouldn't mind giving her Henry. Henry's jolly good comp'ny."

Henry was Jimmy's tortoise, a much prized possession, which Jimmy considered to be endowed with almost superhuman intelligence and charm.

"It's not coloured, like a parrot," objected Bobby. "They're coloured red an' green, are parrots."

"Well, we could colour it," said Jimmy, determined not be turned back by such a slight obstacle as that. "There's green paint in the garage an' there's a pot of red 'namel in the kitchen cupboard."

Bobby shook his head.

"It's not as easy as that," he said. "They talk, do parrots."

"Miss Pettigrew's doesn't."

"Yes, it does. It says 'Miaow!' It's all it can say, but it says it."

"Well, then—" A light broke suddenly over Jimmy's face. "I t-tell you what!"

"Yes?"

"Those kittens of yours!"

Bobby's family cat had, a few weeks ago, given birth to a litter of kittens, for which his mother was still trying to find homes.

"What've they got to do with it?" said Bobby.

"Well, she wants somethin' coloured for comp'ny that says 'Miaow', so we'll paint Henry an' give him to her for – for sort of c-coloured comp'ny, an' we'll give her one of your k-kittens to say 'Miaow'."

Bobby looked at his friend admiringly.

"Gosh! That's a jolly good idea," he said.

"An' I bet she'll be so pleased she'll ring up Daddy an' he'll let Roger go to the circus," said Jimmy.

Then, with the air of one who has solved a difficult problem to the satisfaction of all concerned, he arose from his seat on the wheelbarrow and, accompanied by Bobby, went over to the greenhouse, where Henry, regardless of his doom, was sunning himself among the plant pots. Carried to the garage and thickly coated with red and green paint, Henry proved tractable enough, though there was a dispirited air about him as he stood dripping red and green paint onto the garage shelf.

"He looks jolly fine," said Jimmy, eyeing his handiwork with approval.

"He doesn't look like a parrot," objected Bobby.

"Well, he's not meant to," said Jimmy. "He's meant to be jus' a bit of coloured comp'ny *same* as a parrot. He looks *better* than a parrot to me. If I had to choose between Henry all painted up like this an' a parrot, I'd

choose Henry any day. I bet she won't want that ole parrot back at all, once she's got Henry . . . Come on. We've got to hurry. We'll call for one of your kittens on the way to her cottage."

"We'll take Demon," said Bobby. "It can go on miaowing longer than any of the others. My mother says it's got a voice like a . . ." he paused for a moment, knitting his brows, then ended uncertainly, "syphon."

"A syphon hasn't got a voice," said Jimmy.

"This one had," said Bobby. "Someone told me about her once. She was a witch an' a man in hist'ry didn't want to listen to her singin', so she tied him to a pole an' made him."

"I don't think much of that tale," said Jimmy after consideration. "I'd sooner have Robin Hood or Boadicea any day . . . oh, *come on!*"

They went down the road, Jimmy carrying the still dripping Henry as best he could, and called at Bobby's house for Demon. Demon, a ball of grey fur, allowed himself to be put under Bobby's coat, and they proceeded to Miss Pettigrew's cottage.

Fate seemed to be on their side.

The cottage was empty, the drawing-room window open. The two climbed in at the window, and Jimmy placed Henry in the parrot's cage, while Bobby, on a sudden inspiration, put Demon into Miss Pettigrew's workbox.

"She won't see him at first," he said, "an' it'll be a nice surprise for her when he starts miaowing."

"Yes, that's a jolly good idea," agreed Jimmy. "We want it to be a surprise. She'll enjoy it more if it's a surprise."

It had been arranged that Jimmy should have lunch at Bobby's house, joining his own family in time to go to the circus with them. At Bobby's house, therefore, he ate an ample meal (for anxiety never impaired his appetite), removed as much red and green paint from his person as possible, and hurried home, to find the family all ready to set out. Roger was with them, obviously one of the party.

"Is Roger coming?" said Jimmy, breathless with eagerness.

"Yes, dear," said Mrs Manning.

"D-did Miss Pettigrew ring up?"

"No, dear. Why should she?" said Mrs Manning. "No . . . Your father reconsidered the matter."

She smiled to herself as she remembered the telephone conversation she had had with her husband halfway through this morning.

"I don't for a moment admit that I was in

the wrong," he had said with dignity. "I'm reconsidering the matter simply because the thought of the kid's not going to the circus is putting me off my work. I've lost *pounds'* worth of business through it already, and I can't afford to go on. Don't say anything to him. I intend," he had ended in an impressive, almost magisterial tone of voice, "to have a serious talk with him as soon as I get home."

Mr Manning had begun his "serious talk" with Roger as soon as he got home, but, after reaching a compromise, consisting of the docking of Roger's pocket money, by which the honour of both was satisfied, it degenerated with deplorable rapidity into a discussion on circuses in general and a description of every circus that Mr Manning had ever seen.

"Daddy decided to let him go, after all," said Mrs Manning.

"Oh!" said Jimmy.

He was very thoughtful on his way to the circus . . . He was still thoughtful as he took his seat. He was more thoughtful than ever, as fragments of a conversation carried on by two women in the row behind reached him.

"Poor Miss Pettigrew . . . The room a *shambles*! . . a horrible tortoise in the cage *dripping* red and green paint on to her carpet . . . a frightful cat that had *wrecked* her workbasket and scratched the legs of that lovely table and torn her muslin curtains to shreds . . ."

"What about the parrot?"

"Oh, that came back early this morning, but it seemed nervous of its cage and the drawing room, so she left it loose in her bedroom . . . She says she's going round to every house in the village tomorrow to find out which boy played that wretched trick on her."

Jimmy glanced at his father, who was explaining to Roger how a flying trapeze worked. Oh, well, thought Jimmy, the worst that could happen was soon over. And Roger was at the circus, which was all that really mattered. And tomorrow was a long way off . . . Meantime a little cart was entering the ring, drawn by two dogs and driven by a monkey, who took off his hat with a flourish. Behind came a clown, tripping up at every step . . .

Abandoning himself to the pleasure of the moment, Jimmy gave a yell of delight.

Seventeen Oranges

Bill Naughton

I used to be so fond of oranges that I could suck one after the other the whole day long – until that time the policeman gave me a scare at the dock gates when he caught me almost redhanded with seventeen hidden away in my various pockets, and he locked me up, and ever since then I've never looked at an orange – because that gave me my fill of them.

I was driving a little pony-and-cart for the Swift Delivery Company in those days, and lots of my pick-ups were at the docks, where I could put on a handy sample load and be back at the depot before the other carters had watered their mares.

Now I was not what you call a proper

fiddler, and I did not make a practice of knocking things off just because they didn't belong to me, like some people do, but just the same, it was very rare I came off those docks without a bit of something to have a chew at during the day.

Say they were unloading a banana boat; well, I used to draw my little cart alongside. There were often loose bunches that had dropped off the main stalks. And when the chance came I would either make a quick grab, or some friendly foot would shove them towards me. Then I used to duck them out of sight under my brat. The brat was an apron made from a Tate and Lyle sugar-bag, supposed to be a good protection against rain and rough wear, but mine was used mostly for concealment. And for the rest of that day I'd be munching away at bananas, even though I hadn't a passion for them like I had for oranges.

But mine was all done on the spur of the moment, more or less, and not worked out to a fine art, as in one instance with Clem Jones, who came out of the gates carrying a box.

"What have you got in there?" asked Pongo, who was the bobby on duty.

"A cat," said Clem, "but don't ask me to open it, or the blighter will get away."

"A cat?" said Pongo. "Don't come it. Let's have it opened."

Clem wouldn't at first, but when Pongo insisted he got mad, and he flung it open, and out leapt a ship's cat, which darted back along the docks with Clem after it, shouting. Two minutes later he came out with the same box, holding the lid down tight and scowling at the grinning Pongo, and all the way home he scowled, until in the privacy of his own kitchen he opened the box and took out a full-sized Dutch cheese.

I got caught because the string of my brat broke, and Pongo, after looking over my load, noticed my somewhat bulging pockets. He made me draw the pony-and-cart to one side, and then he took me in his cabin and went through my pockets. There were seventeen oranges in all, and he placed them carefully on the table.

"An example has to be made," he said, "of somebody or other – and I reckon you're the unlucky one. Now, my lad, what have you to say for yourself?"

I said nothing. I was dead frightened, but I forced myself to keep my mouth shut. I had read too many detective stories to make the mistake of blabbing. *Anything you say may be used in evidence against you.* I kept that firm in my mind, and I refused to be interrogated. Pongo, who did not care for my attitude, said,

"Righto, I'll go off and bring a colleague as a witness." And with that he went, carefully locking the door behind him.

I felt awful then. It was the suspense. I looked at the walls, I looked at the door, and I looked at the seventeen oranges, and I looked at my brat with the broken string. I thought of how I would get sacked and get sentenced, and of what my mother would say and my father do.

There was no escape. I was there – and the evidence was there before me on the table – and Pongo had gone for his mate to be witness. I was ruined for life.

"Oh, my God," I moaned in anguish, "whatever shall I do?"

"*Eat 'em!*" spoke a voice in my head.

"Eh?" I asked. "Eat 'em?"

"*Yeh, that's right,*" replied this inner voice "*and then the evidence will be gone. But be quick about it.*"

I thought for half a second – then I snatched an orange, peeled it in a jiff, popped it in my mouth, crushed the juice out and swallowed it, swallowing the orange, and I was just about to squirt out the pips when the voice cried:

"*No!*"

"Eh?"

"*You have to swallow them too!*"

"What – the pips?"

"*Yes – peel an' all! Evidence.*"

"Oh – oh, of course." And I forced the pips to the back of my mouth and took a handful of peel to help get them down my gullet.

"*Don't bother to chew,*" said the voice, "*it's a race against time.*"

It certainly was. After the first orange I took out my penknife and slashed the fruit into chunks and gulped them down as fast as I could pick them up.

I was all but full to the brim, with three oranges still to go, when I heard Pongo and his mate coming back. With a sigh I gave up, but the voice warned me to guzzle on, suggesting that the more I ate the less evidence there would be – and as luck would have it, Pongo and his mate were detained over checking up on some outgoing wagons, and since the sigh seemed to have cleared up a sort of traffic jam in my oesophagus, I set about finishing off those last few, and by the time the key turned in the lock I was consuming the final piece of the seventeen oranges.

"This is him," began Pongo to his mate. "I caught him with his pockets ramjam full of oranges . . ." He looked to the table. "Hi, where are they?"

"Whew," sniffed his mate, "I can smell 'em."

I never spoke.

Pongo began to search. He looked high and low, went through my pockets, felt at my brat, but of course he found no trace of an orange. Finally he figured out what must have happened, but even then he couldn't believe it. "*Seventeen* oranges," he kept murmuring "big 'uns at that! How has he managed it?" But I said nothing. And he couldn't give me in charge, because he had no evidence upon which to commit me – and because I suppose he did not want to be laughed at. So all he could do was vituperate, while I kept my lips shut tight, and then he had to let me go.

When I told Clem Jones about it he said that I had been very slow; he said that I could have sued Pongo for hundreds of pounds because of wrongful detention, if only I had been quick-witted enough. But I never was a vindictive sort, and anyway, it was days and days before I could stand really still and think things out, because those seventeen oranges – peel, pips, and all – kept working away in my inside something shocking.

Fairy Cakes

Moira Miller

They say you should always heed a Fairy's Warning. And it's perfectly true, particularly if they happen to mention the name of Big Katie McCafferty.

She's the same Katie McCafferty who used to run Katie's Cake and Cookie Shop. They came from miles around to buy her treacle and tattie scones. They raved about her plain loaves and morning rolls. But it was the cakes that really made Katie famous. Indeed it was those cakes, and the Wee Folks' fondness for them, that made it possible for her to open the shop at all. This was the way it happened.

Wee Folk generally keep themselves to themselves and eat their own food, but if they have a particular weakness, it is that they are extremely fond of a home-made cake and are not above stealing the odd slice themselves. How often have you gone to the tin and found there's only a small piece left? Who ate the rest? Where did it go? Better not to ask sometimes. But you can be sure if you are a particularly good cake baker then the Wee Folk will get to know about it.

They knew about Katie's cakes and did their very best to get their hands on them. They used to hang around her back door, just in case she left it open a crack, but she never did, she was too clever by half. One morning though, just by chance, one of the Wee Folk happened to be passing when Big Katie had a telephone call.

"It's an order from the castle," she shouted. "The Laird's dochter's to be wed and they want a cake, twelve layers high, with silver bells and white heather. Fancy that, Donnie! I'll hae to leave you wi' Wee James for the day."

"Aye, well just tak' care yir no' too late

coming hame," said her husband Donnie. "It's a lang road through the wood."

"Ach, doesn't bother me!" said Katie. "I'll take the short cut by the Fairy Hill."

"She's to bake the cake in the castle kitchen," panted the fairy who had raced back home with the news. "It'll take her all day, an' she'll gang hame late – by the short cut path round the Fairy Hill!"

In no time at all the Wee Folk had laid a plan to kidnap Katie on her way home from the castle.

"Gin we cannae steal her cakes – we'll steal the cook hersel'!" they screeched with delight. "An' she'll hae tae bide here and bake for us!"

The day of the Cake Baking arrived. After breakfast Katie packed her best apron and prepared to leave.

"Now don't you worry, I'll tak' care o' everything here," Donnie assured her. "But just mind if you're coming home by the Fairy Hill to be back by midnight, yon's no a place to linger late at nicht!"

"No fear of that!" said Big Katie, and off she went.

She spent a long, hot day in the castle kitchen. All morning the little maids ran here and there fetching and carrying, all afternoon they spent washing up behind her. She filled the castle with a mouth-watering smell of fresh-baked fruit and spices. And then, at last, when it was almost bedtime and the Laird and his family could stand it no longer, Katie threw open the kitchen door, and invited them to admire the wedding cake.

It was magnificent. They had never seen one quite like it before. Twelve layers high, each layer standing on little silver pillars and decorated with white heather and bluebells, cleverly moulded from icing. It was so beautiful even the castle cook forgot his huff and invited her to sit down for a cup of tea and bite of supper before she left for home.

"Ah well, just a quick cuppa," said Big Katie, with an eye on the clock. "It's gone ten now, and I must be home before midnight."

But you know how it is, one cup led to

another, they chatted and swapped recipes and in no time at all the kitchen clock was striking half past eleven.

Big Katie grabbed her apron and ran. Down the road from the castle she hurried, over the bridge by the mill to the crossroads.

It was a bright moonlit night, but the long road down through the wood looked dark and eerie with shifting shadows. To her left the short cut path up over the Fairy Hill was bright and beckoning. Stars sparkled like diamonds in the puddles, she could see every step of the way to her own little cottage down in the glen below, where Donnie had left a light in the window.

Ach there's no harm can come to me here, she thought. *I'll just chance it.*

But the hill seemed strangely steeper with every step she took, and as she climbed a great tiredness came over her, so that by the time she was halfway up she was gasping for breath.

"I doubt but I'll hae to sit down here for a wee rest," she said, stretching out on the grass; and in no time at all she had fallen into a deep sleep.

It was the moment the Wee Folk had been waiting for.

Quick as a flash they seized her. She tossed and turned fitfully in her sleep hearing screams and giggles as if in a dream, and opening her eyes found herself in a huge dimly-lit green cave. The laughter came from strange little creatures who seemed to melt in and out of the tree roots around her.

"Well, mercy on us!" she gasped, realizing what had happened. "Whatever am I doing here?"

"Yir here to mak' oor cakes," screeched the little voices. "An' the only wey ye'll get hame is if we tak' ye."

"An' we'll never dae that!" They danced round Big Katie giggling wildly.

"Well, this is a pretty pickle I'm in," she said to herself. "What am I to do, I wonder?" Seeing there was no way of escaping, she sighed, and put on her apron.

"She's going to bake us a cake!" The Wee Folk danced a mad reel. "She's going to bake us a cake."

"Aye, but there's a wee something missing. You've no flour," said Big Katie, searching along the shelves of the fairy kitchen. "You'll have to fetch mine from the cottage." The words were hardly out of her mouth when a fairy was off and back, his wings flapping furiously.

"Here you are," he said. "Now ye can dae it."

"Right enough," said Big Katie. "But – there's a wee something missing. I need six eggs. You'll have to fetch mine . . ." The words were hardly out of her mouth when a fairy was off and back, his wings flapping furiously.

"Six eggs," he said, placing them on the table.

"Aye, that's true," said Big Katie, searching around. "But there's still a wee something missing. It'll be a very dull cake without the sugar. You'll have to . . ." the words were hardly out of her mouth when a fairy was off and back, his wings flapping furiously.

"Sugar," he said, thumping it down on the table. "Now will you make the cake?"

"Make the cake! Bake the cake!" the others chanted, leaping up and down, frantic with excitement.

"Aye, right," she said. "But if it's one of my *special* cakes you want . . ."

"It is! It is!"

". . . there's a wee something missing. One of you will have to fetch my spice jar – it's on the dresser . . ." The words were hardly out of her mouth when a fairy was off and back, his wings flapping furiously.

"Is there anything else?" he gasped, flopping at her feet with the jar.

"Well now – there's milk . . ." Off went another fairy.

". . . and butter. And I think that's just about it," said Big Katie, counting out the ingredients on the kitchen table.

"Make the cake! Bake the cake!" shouted the Wee Folk breathlessly. "Hurry, hurry!"

"Well I would," said Big Katie. "But – there's just a wee something missing. You don't have a baking bowl big enough – you'll have to fetch mine from . . ." The words were hardly out of her mouth when two fairies were off and back, carrying the bowl between them.

"That's more like it," said Big Katie, and she tipped in the flour, and sugar, and eggs, and milk, and spices all ready to mix together. The fairies crowded around her, their tongues hanging out.

"Em – there's just a wee something missing," she said.

"Oh no!" groaned the fairies.

"You don't expect me to stir it with that silly wee spoon do you? You'll find mine . . ." The words were hardly out of her mouth when a fairy was off and back, with the wooden spoon.

"Just the ticket," said Big Katie, and she set to work, mixing the cake.

Slurp, slurp, slurp, slurp, went the spoon in the cake mix.

And then she stopped.

"It's no use. There's just a wee something missing."

"Whit now?" they moaned.

"It's the dog."

"The dog?"

"The dog. I like to have him lying at my feet snoring – it kind of gives me a beat for the mixing."

"Aye, right, the dog," sighed the fairies, and two of them set off to drag back a very unwilling dog, who bit and snapped and snarled.

"Lie down and go to sleep," said Big Katie when they finally got him into the Fairy Hill. The dog lay at her feet and fell asleep.

Snore, snore, snore, went the dog.

Slurp, slurp, slurp, went Big Katie, mixing the cake, soft and moist and brown.

And then she stopped.

"It's not use," she sighed. "There's just a wee something missing."

"Oh no, not again!" sighed the fairies.

"My cat."

"Your cat?"

"Every time I bake a cake he's there, purring at my feet – it just doesna' seem right without him. You'll have to . . ."

"Aye, right, the cat," sighed the fairies, and two of them set off to drag back a very unhappy cat, spitting and scratching and fighting.

"Lie down and go to sleep," said Big Katie when they finally got back to the Fairy Hill, and the cat lay at her feet and fell asleep.

Purr, purr, purr, went the cat.

Snore, snore, snore, went the dog.

Slurp, slurp, slurp, went Big Katie with the wooden spoon.

And then she stopped.

"Don't tell us," howled the fairies. "There's a wee something missing."

"It's the baby," said Big Katie. "He's cutting teeth, and I'm that worried about him." It took four fairies to drag the baby's cot back to the Hill and by the time they got him there, he was wide awake and howling.

"Waaaaa, waaaaa, waaaaa," screamed Wee James.

"Oh, wheeshie whee!" crooned Big Katie.

Snore, snore, snore, went the dog.

Purr, purr, purr, went the cat.

Slurp, slurp, slurp, went the wooden spoon.

"What a din!" howled the fairies, stuffing their fingers in their ears.

Big Katie stopped mixing.

"Tell you what," she shouted. "There's a wee something missing!" She could hardly make herself heard above the row. "Away and fetch my husband. He'll keep the bairn quiet."

Donnie was a big man. It took eight of the fairies to drag him away with his slippers and his newspaper.

"Whit in the name of goodness is going on?" he shouted when they dumped him beside Big Katie. "That hoose is like a fairground tonight, what with all the coming and going . . ."

"Wheesht," she whispered. "Just do as I say

and we'll be all right." She nodded to him to stand on the dog's tail.

"Owowowowow," howled the dog, louder than ever. The cat shot up, screeching and spitting. Wee James screamed at the top of his voice.

The fairies rolled about the floor, howling in agony and begging Katie to stop the noise. But Big Katie ignored them, and clattered the spoon round the bowl.

Slurp, slurp, slurp.

And then she stopped.

"It's ready to bake," she said. The fairies sighed with relief. "But – there's a wee something missing." They screamed and moaned.

"You'll have to fetch my big baking tin . . ." she shouted above the din. Two fairies trudged out, and were back an hour later, rolling the big silver tin between them.

"Bake the cake! Make the cake!" the Wee Folk whispered hoarsely as Big Katie tipped the mix into the tin. "Is that it ready now?"

"Well, yes," said Big Katie. "But . . ."

The Wee Folk rolled around the cave in a howling green bundle.

"Your oven's far too wee for my big cake tin. I can only cook it if you take me . . ." The words were hardly out of her mouth when four fairies grabbed her, another two took the cake tin.

"And don't forget Donnie, and the baby, and the dog, and cat and . . ."

So the Wee Folk spent the rest of that night flapping backwards and forwards between the Fairy Hill and Big Katie's cottage, and didn't she laugh at their faces when they realized that she had tricked them into taking her back home again. You never saw such a miserable bunch of fairies.

In fact they looked so miserable she took pity on them and promised to bake the cake after all. When it was cool, she covered it with lemon icing and took it back up the road to the Fairy Hill.

"Anybody there?" she called, but the only sound to be heard was a faint snoring from deep beneath the earth, so she left the cake and went off back home again.

But that was not the end of the story. Whatever else the Wee Folk do, they will not take something for nothing, so that the very next morning Big Katie found a bag of gold coins on her doorstep. Pinned to the bag there was a note ordering a chocolate cake for the following week. Then after that it was a cream sponge, a strawberry gateau, a green birthday cake. Something different every week.

So you see that was how Big Katie McCafferty was able to make enough gold to open her own wee Cake and Cookie Shop, and why you should always listen to a Fairy Warning. They know when they're beaten.

The Litter Bug

Jamie Rix

In the olden days people never wore trousers. They all wore tights. The reason for this was quite simple. A rat cannot crawl up the inside of a pair of tights, but a trouser leg offers the greatest temptation known to rats, and in the olden days there were rats everywhere. So I ask you, if you had the choice between wearing tights or having a rat up your trousers, which would you choose?

Rats in those days used to be enormous. They would slip out of their ditches or sewers at night and stuff themselves silly on all the rubbish that people threw into the street. The more they ate, the bigger and fatter they became. Some were as big as dogs and roamed the streets in packs. If ever food became hard to find they would attack babies in their prams and chew off their fingers.

Then, one day, a clever man, called Mr Dustbin, realized that if he was ever to get rid of these ferocious rats, he would have to get rid of the rubbish first. So he invented a large bucket into which people could throw their rubbish. Then every Monday he would collect these large buckets and take the rubbish to a secret place where the rats couldn't find it.

The rats soon grew thin and hungry because they had nothing to eat, and in a very short time all the rats in the world died out. Mr Dustbin, however, grew rich and fat on all the money he made from collecting his buckets and retired to a very nice villa in Portugal, where he sat by a swimming pool for the rest of his life and drank beer.

All was well for a hundred years. Then Mr Dustbin died and with him died the memory of the rats. People had forgotten how awful it had been living with those vicious packs of slinky grey nibblers, and they slipped back into their old ways. Litter appeared on the streets again. Empty cans, greasy fish and chip wrappings, old newspapers and broken glass bottles once again lay in festering heaps by the side of the road.

The difference, though, was that this time there were no rats left to eat the rubbish. They had all died because of Mr Dustbin's cunning invention. So the piles of litter just grew bigger. In six weeks city centres throughout the land were overshadowed by vast amounts of plastic food cartons and scrunched up sweet papers. Waves of soggy cardboard boxes, mouldy food and rotting shoes sloshed out of the cities into the countryside, and it was not long before a National Emergency was announced. Great Britain was being buried under a top soil of stinking rubbish.

Schoolchildren were given a shovel and a wheelbarrow and told to clean up the mess. Lessons were cancelled. Classes spent their days rushing to the seaside with wheelbarrows full of rotting waste and dumping the contents into the sea. But it was all to no avail. The litter mountain kept on growing, and all because of one person.

Her name was Bunty Porker. She was as large as a double-decker bus and to all who knew her it was obvious why. She never stopped eating. Thirteen packets of cereal, five pounds of cheese, sixty-four slices of bread and a lorry load of chocolate buttons for breakfast. Eleven packets of crisps for elevenses, and another twelve for twelveses. Then lunch. This was when the serious eating of the day began for Bunty.

Aeroplanes from China flew in her first course. One thousand packets of rice, which she would boil up and serve with a knob of butter on top. This was followed by a vat of frozen peas, as many turkey burgers as she could eat in ten minutes (generally about two hundred), and a microwave full of chips. Pudding was simple. She went down to the local ice cream factory and ate it.

At four o'clock in the afternoon Bunty always felt peckish, so she would make herself some sandwiches. As many as would fit on the kitchen table was usually sufficient, but more often than not she would break into a crate of biscuits and devour those too.

Three hours later it was supper time. Takeaways were her favourite. She would order twelve Indian curries, and ten Chinese set meals for six, then pop down to the local hamburger restaurant for a milkshake and twenty-seven half-pounders with double helpings of everything. And once in bed, a cup of warm milk and a shortbread biscuit to aid digestion.

It was not the vast quantity of food which Bunty ate that was the problem. The litter mountain grew because everything she ate was wrapped in plastic or came in a box, and she had to dispose of the wrappings somewhere.

She made herself a mega-large mackintosh with extra-deep pockets. During the day she filled these pockets with her litter. Come nightfall, she slipped onto the streets and emptied her foul cargo into other people's front gardens, into duck ponds in the park, into bus shelters and shop doorways. Bunty was a litter lout of the most ginormous proportions.

It was not long before the litter mountain was as tall as two mountains. It stretched up through the clouds as far as the eye could see. On the ground its effect was devastating. Lakes disappeared, hills were flattened, cities came to a standstill as the streets clogged up. The country was quite literally a wasteland. People were trapped in their houses and animals buried underground. Bunty was the only person who ever went outside. She was the only person big enough to wade through swamps of old nappies and black banana skins. She was the only person who could stand the foul pong that hung over the land like a damp blanket.

Then the insects came. To them the pong was heaven. It was like waking up in the morning and smelling toast downstairs. The insects couldn't help themselves. One whiff of the litter mountain and they were drawn towards it. They came from all over the world.

Fat flies from America, wolf spiders from Australia, mosquitoes from Africa and big black bugs, the size of fifty pence pieces, from Europe.

It was the Queen who first decided that enough was enough. She rang up the Prime Minister in the middle of the night.

"Yes?" said the Prime Minister sleepily as he sat up in bed.

"Queen here," said the Queen. "What are you going to do about the rubbish? I can't get out to walk the Corgis!"

"Your Majesty," said the Prime Minister, "I had no idea. I'll call a Cabinet meeting straight away and we'll draw up a plan of action."

"You do that," said the Queen, "but hurry. They're only little dogs and they can't hang on much longer."

"Of course," said the Prime Minister. "I'll do everything I can!"

The Cabinet decided that there was only one way to deal with the problem. Catch Bunty.

That night, the army was called in. Twenty thousand troops marched, or rather squelched, into London. The Commanding Officer was a red-faced man with a bristly moustache. His name was Colonel Buffy.

"Leave it all to me, Prime Minister!" he shouted. "My troops have been fully camou-flaged – we've stuck bits of litter in our hats. This Bunty girly will never see us coming. We'll have her locked up within the hour."

Meanwhile, Bunty was not aware that any of this was happening. She was busy stuffing the pockets of her mega-large mackintosh with empty baked bean tins, ready for that night's litter drop.

Bunty left her house as the church clock was striking midnight. The moon was hidden behind a motionless cloud. She bellyflopped into the sticky black river that flowed outside her front door and swam down the road to the foot of the litter mountain. As she heaved herself out of the slime she heard a rustling behind her. She turned to look, but all she could see was litter. She carried on up the mountain. There it was again. That same noise. Only it wasn't just behind her now, it was all around. She peered again through the darkness to see what it was, and this time she definitely saw the rubbish moving. There was something underneath it, trying to push its way out.

"Over here, men," whispered Colonel Buffy. "There she is."

The Colonel pointed at the huge shadowy figure of Bunty standing on the rubbish heap. "You all know what to do. Form a circle round her, then close in and catch her."

"Erm . . . sir," said a weedy soldier, "don't you think she's a bit big for us, sir?"

"Nonsense," said the Colonel, "she's a little girly. No problem." Then he barked, "Forward, men."

Bunty was watching the litter mountain for any further signs of movement. Everything had suddenly gone very quiet and still. The rustling had stopped.

"I must have imagined it," she said to herself. Then she turned and continued climbing.

Suddenly the air was filled with screaming and shouting. There were soldiers everywhere, carrying nets and waving sticks. Litter flew into the air as their heavy boots crashed down the slope towards her. More in terror than bravery, Bunty stood her ground. She was quickly surrounded and held tight by Colonel Buffy's men.

"Bunty Porker?" said the Colonel. "You're a litter bug. You're a menace. You're coming with me."

Bunty looked around at the camouflaged

faces. Twenty thousand soldiers didn't seem that many to her. She turned back to the Colonel.

"Well, actually," she said. "I'd rather not, if you don't mind."

Then she swung her massive arms around her head, until she looked a little bit like a helicopter, and flattened the lot of them.

"Of course," she said to herself as she plodded on up the mountain, "those soldiers must have made that rustling sound, and the moving litter was them crawling towards me! How stupid of me to be scared. Well, at least I can dump my baked bean tins in peace now!"

But Bunty was wrong. The soldiers had been as quiet as mice. Something else had made the rustling sound. Something else had been burrowing away underneath the mountain trying to get out.

Do you remember the rats? The ones that grew into monster rats from eating all the rubbish. The ones that nibbled babies' fingers. They all died out, didn't they? But Bunty's litter mountain had attracted a different kind of visitor. Do you remember the big black bugs from Europe?

As Bunty reached the top of the mountain, she felt something shift under her feet. A long sharp wire pricked her ankle. She jumped backwards. It wasn't a wire. It couldn't be, it was twitching and it was pushing its way out through the side of the mountain. It looked exactly like a feeler on the top of a beetle's head, but that wasn't possible. It was over thirty feet long. No bug was that big . . . Bunty's heart nearly stopped. "Unless the big black bugs from Europe have been eating all the rubbish, and have grown into giant bugs!" she screamed.

The mountainside opened up in front of her. Two enormous black pincers flashed past her head, four leathery wings beat the air and knocked her off her feet. Six hairy legs scuttled out of the hole.

Bunty sat there with her cheeks wobbling and her mouth open. The Litter Bug was hungry. With one enormous gloop, the giant bug sucked up three tons of litter and licked

his lips. Bunty Porker didn't stand a chance. She disappeared along with all the rest of the rubbish.

The Litter Bugs soon ate all the litter and Bunty's mountain was reduced to a mere compost heap within a month. When the rubbish ran out, the Litter Bugs flew away in search of food elsewhere, but people had learnt their lesson. They never threw litter onto the street again. They always put it in a dustbin, as Mr Dustbin had taught them to, all those years before.

ACKNOWLEDGEMENTS

The publishers wish to thank the following for permission to reproduce copyright material.

George Layton: "The Balaclava Story" from *Northern Childhood: The Fib and Other Stories* by George Layton; first published by Longman 1975 and Macmillan Children's Books 1997 and reproduced by permission of Pearson Education Ltd.

Penelope Lively: "Nat and the Great Bath Climb" from *A House Inside Out* by Penelope Lively and copyright © Penelope Lively 1987; first published by Puffin Books 1989 and reproduced by permission of Penguin Books Ltd.

Marcus Crouch: "Ivan's Shadow" from *Stories of Old Russia* by Marcus Crouch; first published by Oxford University Press 1989 and reproduced by permission of O.M. Crouch.

John Agard: "Anyone for a Banana?" by John Agard; reproduced by permission of Caroline Sheldon Literary Agency on behalf of the author.

William Raeper: "The Reluctant Dragon and the Wilful Princess" from *The Troll and the Butterfly* by William Raeper and copyright © William Raeper 1987; first published by Andre Deutsch 1987 and reproduced by permission of Rogers, Coleridge & White Ltd.

Bill Naughton: "A Good Sixpenn'orth" and "Seventeen Oranges" from *The Goalkeeper's Revenge and Other Stories* by Bill Naughton; first published by Harrap 1961 and reproduced by permission of Thomas Nelson & Sons Ltd.

Helen Cresswell: "Particle Goes Green" from *Winter's Tales for Children Four* by Helen Cresswell and copyright © Helen Cresswell; reproduced by permission of A.M. Heath & Co. Ltd on behalf of the author.

Richmal Crompton: "A Question of Grammar" from *Just – William*; first published by George Newnes 1922 and Macmillan Children's Books 1990. "Miss Pettigrew's Parrot" from *Jimmy* by Richmal Crompton; first published by George Newnes 1949 and as *Just Jimmy* by Macmillan Children's Books 1998. Both stories reproduced by permission of A.P. Watt Ltd on behalf of Richmal Ashbee.

James Thurber: "The Night the Bed Fell" from *My Life and Hard Times* by James Thurber and copyright © James Thurber 1933, 1961; reproduced by permission of The Barbara Hogenson Agency Inc by arrangement with Rosemary A. Thurber.

Ruth Manning-Sanders: "The Good Ogre" from *A Book of Ogres and Trolls* by Ruth Manning-Sanders; first published by Methuen 1972 and reproduced by permission of David Higham Associates Ltd on behalf of the Estate of Ruth Manning-Sanders.

Robert Leeson: An extract from *Harold and Bella, Jammy and Me* by Robert Leeson and copyright © Robert Leeson 1980; reproduced by permission of Egmont Children's Books.

Paul Jennings: *The Paw Thing* by Paul Jennings; first published by Puffin Books and copyright © Paul Jennings 1989; reproduced by permission of Penguin Books Australia Ltd.

Robert Leeson: "Oonagh" from *Smart Girls Forever* by Robert Leeson and copyright © Robert Leeson 1996; reproduced by permission of Walker Books Ltd.

Moira Miller: "Fairy Cakes" from *A Kist O' Whistles* by Moira Miller and copyright © Moira Miller 1990; first published by Andre Deutsch 1990 and reproduced by permission of Scholastic Ltd.

Jamie Rix: "The Litter Bug" from *Grizzly Tales for Gruesome Kids* by Jamie Rix and copyright © Jamie Rix 1990; first published by Andre Deutsch and reproduced by permission of Scholastic Ltd.

Every effort has been made to trace the copyright holders but if any have been inadvertently overlooked the publishers will be pleased to make the necessary arrangement at the first opportunity.